In The Dark

By

Tamara Arts

www.DarkInkBooks.com

*For the ones who believe that there is
just a little more than we can see.*

Chapter 1

Lea

I thanked God that this house was sturdy, and the wood didn't creak under my feet as I crossed the landing.

The rain plagued the windshield of the car. From the shaking of the vehicle, I could tell that the road was full of bumps and holes. The air was getting grim, and I feared the worst. With my hand I clasped the handle of the door. *I'm going to die*, I thought as I looked out the window, straight into the abyss. Kai sat hunched over and with half-closed eyes next to me at the wheel. *Please let him get us to our destination safely. Don't let the road be too slippery, don't let us plummet down.*

Ashley placed her small hands on my shoulders, startling me. "Lea, didn't you say the weather would be nice this week?"

I glanced in the rearview mirror, but only saw her long blonde hair next to my headrest. "According to the weather report, yes, but that app can't be trusted half the time. It just goes to show," I sighed shakily. I had chosen this week so carefully, waited until the last moment to be sure it was ideal vacation weather; sunny, reasonably warm and dry.

"I could have told you that as well, couldn't I?" Ashley curled her blonde hair around her finger.

I opened my mouth to say something, but Jill beat

me to it. "You could have looked at a few weather sites yourself. Don't put all the blame on Lea." She rolled her eyes irritably, then leaned forward and sweetly raised the corner of her mouth. "You look a little pale, Lea. Are you okay?" If Jill kept being so piqued at Ashley, it wouldn't be long before the boys caught on to something.

Dennis, who was sitting between the two girls, laughed and said, "When doesn't Lea look pale? She really reminds me of Casper the ghost sometimes." At that, he received a poke in the side from Ashley.

I consciously decided to ignore him for now and turned my head to Jill so I wouldn't have to look outside. Behind her short brown hair, I could only see rocks through the window; on my side was a precipice. If Kai missed a turn, steered a little too far to the right, or the wheels slipped in this mud, we would fall dozens of feet. We would be crushed. And then how long would it take for us to be found? "Yeah, right. I'm fine," I squeaked. I couldn't reassure myself, but I realized that perhaps I should have more faith in my boyfriend's driving skills.

"You haven't looked at the weather reports yourself, have you? So you aren't allowed to speak on the matter," Ashley responded, totally ignoring our words, to Jill's comment.

"But I'm not the one sitting here whining," Jill bounced back.

Ashley crossed her arms and frowned. "I'm not doing that either!"

"Stop it, please!" Yelled Kai in a heavy voice. "I'm

trying to concentrate. Or would you rather I drive off the road and we crash?" A drop of sweat dripped down his temple.

Ashley and Jill fell silent and both looked the other way. As the rain started to get heavier and heavier and the wind pounded against the side of the car, I realized that this week was probably not going to be such a blast. For the past few days, the two had been constantly bickering. And only I knew why. The guilt wracked me up inside.

To distract myself, I focused on Kai. The muscles under my boyfriend's dark skin tightened every time he had to go through a turn. His fingers clasped the steering wheel tightly. He had had his driver's license for over a year now - the only one in our group, since he was a year older - and drove us everywhere. He was so attractive when he drove a car. Normally I would run my fingers over his forearm, but since he had to concentrate pretty hard right now and I wanted to stay alive, I didn't.

"Wow, is that the house?" Dennis, who was sitting in the middle at the back, bent down so that his face was right next to mine.

I squeezed my eyes to slits. It was too dark to see more than a few vague outlines at the end of the dirt road. "I think so, I can't see very well."

"Honey?" Dennis nudged Ashley. "Is that the house your parents showed you?" For someone with his physique, he still had a fairly high-pitched voice. Jill and I always joked that puberty had skipped him.

"Yes!" cried Ashley after a while. She clapped her

hands briefly.

Relieved, I let myself fall backwards into the passenger seat. Finally. The closer we got, the more details I could discern. In the distance, I could see the outline of a house, but now that we were so close, all I could see was fencing. The fence reached at least eight feet high and thick climbing plants grew between the bars, so I couldn't see through them. The greenery spread upward and to the sides; the yard looked neglected. Did no one maintain this garden?

Kai stopped the car just before the gate and I had to crane my neck to make out the top of it. What was such a high fence for?

Behind me I heard Ashley fumbling with a pair of keys, then she opened the door and said, "All right then!"

Through the car window, I saw her small stature running toward the gate. Her hands were in front of her face to protect herself from the rain. She put the key in the lock and gave a tug on the gate. It didn't budge. Ashley pulled and pushed a few more times. Slowly she became completely soaked and her blonde hair stuck to her face. She gestured that she needed help.

"Hopefully we really aren't made of sugar." Dennis was the first to come to the rescue. However, the gate appeared to be clamping down considerably, as they needed our help as well.

Jill sighed before stepping out into the pouring rain. I followed.

"Here, let me do it." After Jill pulled vigorously on the gate a few times, it opened with creaking hinges.

The peeling green paint clung to Jill's hands as she let go of the contraption. My breath caught at the sight of the house.

Kai drove out into the yard in front of us.

"Great, Ashley. What a beautiful lie you have told us," Jill said, meanwhile patting her hands off. "This isn't a nice family home to spend our vacation in, it's a ruin."

"Hey, don't look at me! My parents said this was ideal." She curled her blonde hair around her index finger and chewed on it nervously.

"Yeah, a hundred years ago maybe!"

As soon as I took a step into the yard, a shiver slid down my spine. Their bickering faded into the background. My arm muscles cramped and I remained standing. It made sense that it was so foggy in the mountains, but not when it was raining or when the fog didn't reach higher than my ankles. The lack of sunlight gave the house an ominous look. The shutters that hung in front of the windows were as rotten as the wood around them. The black spots were visible from here. Because of the way the windows and the middle of the house were built, it looked like a face watching me. I felt the eyes burning on me. The house towered so high above me that I felt like a rat in a trap. That feeling was amplified when I heard the gate behind me clicking in the lock and Ashley turning the key. My gaze slowly scanned the rest of the property. It was truly huge. Behind the house, the yard stretched dozens of feet, if not hundreds. The trees I could see in the distance bent with the wind. The house was the centerpiece of the land that was within these fences.

I shook off the unpleasant feeling - it was only a house, after all - and strode toward the ruin. There was no better description for this wreck. Why Ashley's parents recommended this place to us was beyond me.

It seemed to be raining harder by the second and I wanted to get inside as quickly as possible, where it was dry.

"So... I'm not listening to your parents anymore," Dennis said, walking beside Ashley. He had put his firm arm around her.

She looked up at him. "You as well? You'll have to, sweetheart, if you want to take another step across the threshold of our house."

"Of course I still want to feel welcome, but you must admit that this is not exactly a place where I want to spend two weeks of my summer vacation," he said. I could only agree with him. Not only the house itself, but also the rain spoiled the vacation feeling. As if we weren't welcome here.

"I agree with Dennis. Besides, this house doesn't seem to be standing firmly at its seams. This place even seems dangerous," I added to the conversation. "What if the roof collapses?"

"Don't get carried away. I'm sure it looks a lot better inside. Come on, I need to go to the bathroom."

I sighed. Ashley and her far too small bladder had been a problem on the road, too. According to my calculations and the navigation system, the car ride took four hours. But thanks to the many pee breaks we had to take for her, we had ended up taking five hours. And then the bad weather kicked in as well.

Kai got our suitcases out of the car and I walked up to him.

"Don't you think this house is creepy?" I immediately asked.

He glanced up at the house. "It is indeed not a pretty thing."

That wasn't what I meant, but I left it at that. I guess I was the only one who was so paranoid. Part of me considered asking to get out of here, but I couldn't do that. We had all been so looking forward to this vacation and now it was finally here. For the first time without parents or siblings.

When everyone had packed their bags, we walked to the front door. The house was made of stone, but the door was built with the same wood as the window frames. The transition from the stone to the doorframe consisted of a huge gap. I wrinkled my nose. That had to be draughty. It didn't exactly look insulated.

Jill, who had taken the keys from Ashley earlier because she didn't think things were moving fast enough, put the key in the lock and pounded on the front door. The door swung open and a cloud of dust welled up. Jill stumbled and fell inside.

"Well, at least it's open," I muttered. A tickle entered my nose and we all had to cough.

"Did you bring your dust mite allergy pills, Lea?" asked Kai. He waved some dust away that had gathered in front of my face.

"Thank goodness I did," I sighed.

Jill reappeared in the doorway and threw her arms

in the air. "Ladies and gentlemen, I'm alive." A layer of dust lay on her short brown hair.

"Too bad," Dennis said.

Jill teasingly stuck out her tongue, grabbed her bags and walked into the house. We went after her. It was blowing so hard that I struggled to push the door closed against an invisible shield of wind. As soon as it fell into the lock, it was suddenly very quiet and dark in the house. I could hear the blood whizzing in my ears, the creaking of planks around me. My eyes had to get used to the dark and my nose was still itching from the dust. I could make out vague outlines of furniture, walls and openings, but otherwise I had to make do by touch.

"We need to open those shutters," Kai remarked. He groped his way down the wall toward the nearest window. I could just make out his tall figure in the shadows. After some creaking and scrambling, light finally came into the room. The wind immediately whizzed through the house, bringing raindrops with it. Kai's upper body hung outside the window, as the shutter had to be attached to the outside wall. After a few seconds, he closed the window and it was silent again.

"So, at least now I can see something," Kai said.

"Um, are you still living in the twentieth century?" Dennis grabbed his phone and activated the flashlight function. "We have these things these days, did you know?"

"Get out of here," Kai sighed. Despite his exasperated undertone, I saw the corners of his mouth briefly pull up into a smile.

"Gladly! Come, Ashley, we'll sort out our room in advance while they bathe the ground floor in light," Dennis said theatrically. He grabbed her hand and pulled her with him up the stairs. Not much later they disappeared out of sight.

"Three guesses what those two are going to do up there." Jill wiggled her eyebrows suggestively.

I laughed while shaking my head. "As if you wouldn't have done the same if your girlfriend had been allowed to come along. Besides, if it's creaking up there as bad as it is down here we don't even have to guess." I looked at Kai with a pained facial expression. He shrugged in response.

Jill, Kai and I went around the ground floor to open all the shutters. The abundant light gave me a chance to take a closer look at the room. Despite the layer of dust, it indeed wasn't too bad inside. There was enough furniture for the five of us and at the dining table there was room for six. The kitchen, however, left much to be desired. The dark wood in combination with the furniture that could have come straight from the house of the Salvatore brothers in *The Vampire Diaries* - dark brown leather sofas - made it look darker than it was. The house seemed so old that I wondered if they had electricity here at all. Well, at least the roof didn't leak. We just had to make the best of it.

Jill styled her hair with her fingers and picked up her bags. "Yo, I'm on my way to my room."

"Let's find a room too and put our stuff there. Then we'll go over everything with a cloth," Kai said.

"Thoroughly," I agreed. My nose was still itching. I

had been about to sneeze for a few minutes, but it wouldn't come out.

Two arms grabbed me from behind. I was startled, but as soon as I saw the dark brown skin tone, I relaxed. I was so focused on the house that I hadn't noticed that my boyfriend had come up behind me. "Kai, you scared me."

He smiled and pressed a kiss to my cheek. "Mission accomplished." His smile still gave me tingles in my stomach.

Grinning, I detached myself from his embrace, then picked up my bags. I looked at him out of the corner of my eye. What I saw certainly didn't hurt my eyes. His thin arm muscles tightened as he had to apply force to lift the suitcases. I bit my lower lip and looked away when he caught my gaze. The jitters flew even higher, which was immediately accompanied by guilt.

"Let's go and look for our room. Since Mr. and Mrs. left us right away," I said quickly.

As soon as we got upstairs, it appeared that Ashley and Dennis had already opened the shutters. The landing was filled with fresh mountain air, and the light allowed me to see the dust floating through the room. On the left and right sides of the hallway were three doors. According to Ashley, there were two bedrooms and a bathroom on each side. The bathroom was in the middle and could also be entered through the bedrooms, but luckily the bathroom doors could be locked.

"There you are!" Ashley came running out of one of the left rooms. "Come, choose yours." She went ahead of us to the one on the far right at the back. "This is the second largest, so that one is for Lea and Kai. The other one is smaller, so you can have that one, Jill."

Well, there was little to choose from.

I only noticed that Jill was standing behind us when she said, "That's not fair." Jill dropped her bags and put her hands to her sides. "You and Dennis certainly have the biggest one?"

"Of course, this house belongs to my family, and we were here first."

"And what about this one?" Jill pointed to the room that hadn't been listed as an option.

"Oh, that one is just for junk. A storage room for old junk. I don't think you want to sleep among that."

Jill heaved a sigh and hummed that she was okay with Ashley's earlier division.

"Nice, make yourself at home."

Our room was indeed fairly large. There was a wooden bed between two windows and a closet. The door to the bathroom and the mirror set up against the opposite wall meant that there were few opportunities to fill the walls. The corners of the room were shrouded in shadow partly because of the dark wood. The spiders apparently also thought this was a good room to settle in. Everywhere I looked there were webs hanging. I stayed away from those. What struck me was that it was also quite cold in this room. Carefully, I placed my suitcases next to the closet. I ran a finger over the carved wood and immediately it was covered in dust.

"Hopefully we brought enough cleaning solution,"

I said. I had no intention of suffering from my dust allergy for a week and pushing all kinds of pills down my throat.

"You took care of all the shopping yourself, Lea. So yes, if anyone knows, it's you." Kai dropped onto the bed and placed his hands behind his head. He followed me with his eyes as I inspected the room.

"You're right. I got everything according to plan and if we don't have enough, we'll go to the store in the nearest village. You have a car, so you can drive. And should any problems arise, in any way, we always have our phones to..."

"Lea!" chuckled Kai. "Take it easy. Everything went well, didn't it? Granted, the state of the house is a setback and the weather could have been better, but we still have a roof over our heads. And since you've taken care of the much-needed stuff, I have no doubt that it's perfect."

He got up from the bed, came to stand in front of me and crossed his arms. He wasn't much taller than me, about five inches at most. But what could I say? I was rather tall for a girl.

I copied his posture and looked straight at him. "How much faith you have in me."

Smiling, he put his arms around me. I pressed my nose into his neck and sniffed his wonderful scent. As always, he took every opportunity to put his arms around me for a moment.

His hands went caressingly over my lower back and he sighed contentedly into my neck.

Even though the house was straight out of a

horror movie, with Kai and my friends around me it was bound to be a fun vacation.

Chapter 2

Dennis

Every time he entered the room it was as if the air had become a little more static, the world outside even darker.

The rest of the morning we thoroughly took care of the house. Man, what a crap job that was. All that dust and grime... While the smell of spaghetti sauce filled the house a little later, I sat with Ashley and Jill waiting for lunch to be prepared by our responsible couple. Lea thought it would be better to eat warm food in the afternoon, only for today, since the trip had been pretty tiring after all and we'd get more energy this way. Okay, Mom.

"Come on with the food," I groaned. "I'm starving!" With my hand I patted my belly a few times.

"Patience!" yelled a male voice from the kitchen.

Jill leaned her head on her arms on the table. "You're not the only one. We all have stomachs that need filling." By the sound of her tone I could tell she was bothered by something. Surely it wouldn't still be about her being assigned the smallest room? She was my best friend and I knew her inside out, yet sometimes I didn't understand anything about her. Or girls in general, it seemed to me.

"Are you hangry now as well?" asked Ashley.

Jill raised her eyebrow. "Hangry? You make up

those words on the spot, don't you?"

"That's not true, it's been used in English for a long time. It's the combination of hungry and angry."

"I'm not angry at all."

Ashley snorted, ready to say something back.

I tried to ignore their bickering as best I could. When Jill broke up with Ashley, their friendship had remained intact, though it took a while for everything to go back to normal in our group. The two did clash, but the last few days they had been acting very hostile to each other. Ashley was her passive-aggressive self and Jill was rather straightforward. How did I choose between the girl I was in love with and my best friend?

"You don't seem very happy either," Ashley insisted.

"Of course not. I have to spend two weeks in a rundown house. That's different from what you had said. Is there a TV? No. Is there a phone signal? No. There's nothing here at all!"

"How many times do I have to tell you that's not my fault? You knew there would be no Wi-Fi or television. What do you want me to do? Call my parents to tell them we're coming home...in the middle of a storm?"

Jill crossed her arms and looked the other way, annoyed. "No, but you can let them know that their idea of 'vacation home' is a little different than what we've encountered."

"Give it a rest," I interjected into the conversation. "We haven't even been inside for two hours and you're already arguing." As soon as the words left my mouth, I knew I would have been better off not saying anything. I never learned. But what was going on with those two anyway?

Ashley sprung up. "Let it rest? You're supposed to take my side!"

"Oh yeah?" Jill stood up so fast it made even me dizzy. "I'm his best friend!"

I ran my hands through the blonde curls that had fallen before my eyes. "Wow, I'm not taking anyone's side. I care about both of you."

"But I'm your girlfriend, or doesn't that mean anything to you?" asked Ashley.

"What? No. I mean yes. Or..." I puffed. How could I get myself out of this? "I'm in a relationship with you now, but we've all been in the friend group for the same amount of time. That's what I meant."

"Are you sick of me?"

"What?" It seemed like that was the only word I could say right away. "No, of course not."

"But you have got that tone in your voice," Ashley said. She pulled a pout, quickly twisting her blonde hair around her fingers.

"That's because I want to have a nice vacation, man, without this." With arm gestures, I tried to make it clear that 'this' meant their bickering.

Jill chuckled sarcastically. "That's exactly why I broke up with you, Ash."

"Jill!" I shouted in shock. We always made fun of each other, but now she was out of line.

"It's like that, isn't it? All that whining about whether I was sick of her and now it's your problem."

"That's not true!" Ashley stood up and walked towards her. "We broke up because you always have to have your way."

"Yes, just like you do," she retorted. They stood face to face and Jill towered over Ashley's small stature. With her hands at her sides, Jill tried to make it clear that she was in charge of this discussion.

If Ashley was a cartoon character, steam would be coming out of her ears right now. She was running red. One of them would have been better off staying home. Somehow I would have preferred Jill to go on vacation with her own girlfriend and her family. Hopefully this wouldn't be the case for the entire vacation, since it looked like we were stuck in this house for the time being thanks to the weather.

"Jill," I interjected.

"What?" they shouted in unison.

"Can you go into the kitchen and see how Kai and Lea are doing? Please." With my eyes I tried to make it clear that it wasn't a question, but an order.

She visibly hesitated between following my advice and going against it, because normally she didn't just do what someone else said. Rather the opposite. Finally, she walked complainingly to the kitchen. On the way she mumbled something under her breath, something Ashley apparently picked up with her sharp ears. In a split second, Ashley turned and dashed toward Jill. But before she actually got to her, I grabbed her arm and stopped her.

"I didn't think so," I said. I didn't give her a chance to say more and escalate this situation. I had had enough. Ashley was known as someone who sometimes made sharp comments, but by now I had learned that it was purely to mask her insecurity. Still, sometimes it could be taken down a notch. "Listen, I love you. Okay? But please stop provoking people."

"That's not what I was doing."

"Then what was it?"

She apparently had nothing to say to that. I didn't know what made her behave that way today, but I noticed that she was mostly taking it out on Jill. Had something happened between the two of them in the meantime? No, she would tell me. Although... Oh well, I shouldn't behave so weird. I'm sure it was just girl stuff. Between exes.

At that moment Lea came out of the kitchen with Kai and Jill behind her. She called us for dinner as she set the steaming pan on the dining table.

Water ran into my mouth as I sat down on the chair. From sitting in the car all day, the disappointment of our vacation destination, and the storm, we were all pretty tired.

I grabbed a spoon and scooped up a large pile of spaghetti with tomato sauce. I sniffed the air, which smelled like the delicious food in front of us, and it seemed like the smell went straight through my nose to my stomach, because it immediately started to growl.

Lea looked at me with raised eyebrows. "Please, eat," she chuckled.

"It smells so good! Just be careful, Kai. I'll be stealing your girlfriend for her cooking very soon. Just kidding, honey," I said quickly after I saw Ashley's gaze.

Lea's blue eyes began to twinkle and she tucked her russet hair into a ponytail. "Thanks, it's a family recipe."

"It looks like regular tomato sauce to me." Ashley took a bite. "But it's delicious," she agreed.

"Very tasty, Lea," Jill confirmed with a smile. So those two could agree on something after all.

Kai pointed his fork around the group. "What about me? I was helping."

"Yes, you stood next to me and watched," Lea laughed. Kai nudged her gently with his shoulder and smiled his familiar smile. Immediately I saw a blush appear on Lea's cheeks.

Unbelievable. Those two had been together for almost two years and still they had that effect on each other. Did Ashley and I still have that too? After a year, there weren't as many jitters as there were in the beginning. Was that normal? I'm sure it was.

I took a few big bites of my food and I had to say...Lea's cooking skills were almost better than my mom's. Almost.

As I ate, my eyes slid to the shadows in the living room. It was the middle of the day, but it might as well have been the middle of the night. A breeze blew through the house and I shivered from the cold mountain air. A bang echoed through the house, causing me to spill the water all over my pants from the shock. "Fuck."

Ashley's hand lingered in the air on the way to the food. "What was that?" With her eyes she searched for mine. Mine were drawn to the stairs.

Before I could say anything, Jill said, "It came from upstairs." We looked at each other with wide eyes and quickly I counted my friends to assure myself that we were all in the dining room.

We remained stiffed in our seats, none of us uttering a word. I could even hear the swishing of blood in my ears, but upstairs it now remained silent.

"Ugh, what if there's a burglar?" I wiggled my eyebrows and looked at Ashley smiling broadly.

She punched my shoulder. "That's not funny! What if there really is someone there?" With wide eyes, she looked around the group.

"Probably an open window and something was blown away by the wind," Kai suggested.

"Exactly. Let's continue eating..." Boom. I shot a few inches into the air and my heart missed a beat. Ashley let out a shriek.

It was probably a window, like Kai said. Now that I had recovered from the shock, a plan formed in my head. I grabbed my chance. "I'll go take a look." I hoped to give them a good scare. Dilapidated house, the darkness of the storm...ideal. Man, this was going to be a fun vacation. The possibilities piled up in my head.

No one stopped me as I walked towards the stairs. It wasn't until I had walked up the first few steps that I wondered if it was really windows we had heard. I breathed in and out deeply. *Come on, scaredy-cat*, I thought. *Put some pep in your step and go for it.*

At the top of the stairs, the bang echoed again, but this time it was a lot louder. It was coming from Ashley and mines room. It was so dark on the landing that I couldn't see very far. As I stepped into the darkness, I felt my palms get damp. With a pounding heart, I snuck into the room where the sound was coming from. As soon as I reached the doorway of our room, I found out the cause. With a confident heart I walked into the room and headed straight for the window. And yes, indeed. Another bang. It was the shutter being blown open and closed by the strong wind. The bangs we heard were coming from the shutter being thrown against the outside wall.

I pulled the window open inward and then I hung my upper body over the windowsill to get the hatch. The rain slapped in my face and the wind blew my hair in front of my eyes, so I couldn't see anything for a while.

Behind me I heard the crunch of footsteps on the wooden floor. "Were you worried about me after all, Ash?" I smiled wearily. She didn't say anything, but I felt the presence behind me. A moment later, I felt her hand on my lower back. "Wow, Ash, you almost pushed me out the window." I balanced dangerously between inside and outside, but finally managed to pull the shutter towards me. A grin appeared around my lips and I pulled the shutter closed extra hard. I laughed out loud when, in response, I heard a few shrieks from below and the feeling of the hand disappeared.

I pinned the thing to the inside wall.

"Yes! They got quite a scare." I turned around expecting Ashley to try and lecture me. However, the room was dark and empty. That was odd, I hadn't heard her walk away. I shrugged. The wind and rain in my ears were pretty loud. I left it at that.

"So, what was it?" Ashley asked, wide-eyed, when I was back downstairs. Her concern was touching. And misplaced.

"A shutter that was blown against the wall by the wind. Nothing exciting. But you already knew that, didn't you?" I winked.

Ashley looked at me like she didn't know what I was talking about. "How would I know?"

Was she kidding me?

"Because you... Never mind."

The rest nodded and I thought I saw relief on their faces. I took a seat and immediately began to continue eating, half aware of the presence I also felt upstairs.

Chapter 3

Ashley

"You were having sex with someone else behind my back!"

As I rubbed the ring on my finger, I watched as the storm only seemed to increase. Thanks to this weather, we were locked in this hovel for the time being. The trees that surrounded the house were blown briskly in one direction and leaned over dangerously far. Leaves were blowing across the yard. Even in the hallway I had noticed the wind blowing through the crack. I let my head hang down defeated. For now, I would not be lying in the sun to get a nice tan.

Behind me I heard laughter. Jill and Dennis were once again being secretive.

As I watched their surreptitious whispering, I asked, "What are you two up to this time?"

They looked up quickly. "Nothing." Dennis laughed innocently. I rolled my eyes. Yeah, sure.

Goosebumps appeared on my arms as a gust of wind blew through the house. With my hands I rubbed my arms. It was getting darker and colder. Surely the heater was on? I walked over to the nearest heater and put my hand on it, after which I immediately hissed as I pulled it back. Yes, it was definitely on. Huh, now I had a little burn, too. Just perfect.

"Shall we go and see what we're going to do for

the next few days?" Lea's voice pulled me out of my thoughts. "Now that it's storming we need to adjust our vacation to-do list accordingly."

"Man, do we have to do that now?" Dennis groaned.

I nodded in agreement. I didn't feel like looking at that right now either. That only reminded me of the fact that we had nothing to do for the next few days. I would have preferred sun, sea, and beach, but since we were poor students and our parents also didn't have the means to pay for their own vacation as well as ours, the best outcome was to pay a visit to my family's inherited house. And it seemed that the five of us were the first persons after decades to visit. My parents, as to my knowledge, had never been here either. I remembered that when we got the news that the house was being passed on to them after my grandmother died, they were afraid that they didn't have the time or money to maintain this house. The only thing they had done was hire someone to connect electricity and heating, but they hadn't been there themselves.

"Yes, I'll get my phone." Lea got up and walked to a corner of the room, where she clicked on a lamp. "Wait a minute. Where's my phone?" she turned to us. "Who took it?"

I looked up at her. Lea who lost her phone? No way. If she could, she would keep a list of what was where at what time. Maybe she did. Her gaze fell on me.

"Hey, don't look at me. I didn't even know there was a table there, let alone that your phone was on it," I defended myself. The look of silent panic spread across her face.

"Didn't you take it with you to your bedroom?" Dennis, who hung nonchalantly on the sofa, asked. His blond curls hung half in front of his eyes, so I couldn't tell if he was serious or if he had something to do with the disappearance of her phone.

Lea's chest was rising and falling more and more violently. "No, it can't be. I'm sure it was right here. Really none of you took it?"

Kai got up as soon as he noticed Lea starting to panic. Rubbing her back reassuringly, he said" "Calm down. Your phone hasn't got legs, you'll find it."

Dennis shook his head. "Maybe it was a ghost," he laughed. He made a haunting sound. Lea's head turned in his direction, then she lowered herself into a squat and continued searching on the ground. "Relax, you don't believe in that stuff, do you?"

"Of course not," she muttered. Pretty soon she was back on her feet. "Seriously, Dennis. This is something you'd do. Give me my phone."

He and Jill exchanged a look. And there you had it. That sneaky laughter from earlier. Apparently, I wasn't the only one who noticed.

"I don't have it, I swear." Dennis put on his most innocent face. Jill joined him. I loved Dennis, but sometimes I got very tired of his jokes. They knew as well as anyone else that this was exactly what you shouldn't do to Lea.

When I saw something glistening on the couch behind Dennis, I ran up to him. Before he knew what I was doing, I snatched the thing from behind him. He made a frantic attempt to snatch the phone back, but it failed. Immediately I heard a relieved sigh behind me. I handed Lea her phone, after which she thanked me.

"Not funny," she told Dennis and Jill. Her eyes spewed fire, but those flames quickly disappeared and gave way to resignation. She plopped back down on the couch next to Kai.

I followed her lead and sat down next to my own boyfriend.

Jill, who was sitting across from me, crossed her arms and looked at me from under her eyelashes. "You always have to ruin it," she muttered.

"Who, me?" Where was this coming from? Normally she was so nice, she was there for everyone, but since our...incident she has become downright a bitch to me. Where is that nice girl with spirit who got along with everyone and laughed at everything? Who comforted me when something was wrong and with whom I could call until two o'clock in the night when I didn't feel well?

"Yes, you. We can't even have some fun; you always get in the way."

"I'm sorry, but didn't you see that Lea almost panicked? I was just trying to help a friend," I said indignantly.

"You have several friends, you know. Besides, it wasn't that bad for Lea. Everyone loses their phone from time to time." Jill made it even worse. "You've just got to make such a big deal about everything now."

Dennis kept quiet, which would normally be the

right thing to do, but right now I needed him. Out of the corner of my eye, I watched him press his lips together, as if he literally had to restrain himself from saying anything. Thanks for that.

"You know Lea! She always has everything in control, she panics when things suddenly go wrong," I shouted. I balled my hands into fists and the nails dug in my palms.

"Well, it's not that bad," Lea said softly. "Really, it's not that big of a deal." Her words went completely past me.

But not past Jill, because she said, "See? You're making a mountain out of a molehill."

"Me?! You're the one who's been acting like a bitch towards me ever since we... At least I'm still trying to act normal. Friendly."

Dennis placed a hand on my knee. "Calm down, Ashley."

"Calm down?" The fire inside me flared up. And he chose this moment, these words, to stand by me? "I won't calm down until she knows her place!"

"And I won't calm down until you know yours!" Jill jumped up from her chair. I could see it in her eyes, in the way her lips moved apart. With my gaze, I tried to stop her from uttering the words, but it was too late. "Do you know what your place is? With your boyfriend, not with me!" She spoke the words in such a way that their meaning could not be missed.

An adrenaline rush shot through my body. No, she did not just say that. She couldn't do that. All the blood drained from my face as Lea inhaled heavily. I felt

Dennis stiffen beside me. It took Jill a moment to realize what she had said. All the anger disappeared from her face and gave way to disbelief. She slapped a hand in front of her mouth.

"I... Dennis..." she stammered.

My lips moved apart, ready to say something, but my vocal cords were not cooperating. Had she been planning all along to throw it into the group like that? She couldn't. Then she would lose her best friend, too. She and Lea had promised me not to tell anyone.

Dennis cleared his throat. "What do you mean 'not with me'?" His eyes were fixed on Jill. She slumped back in her chair.

My heart was beating wildly in my chest. Was I supposed to speak up? Jill was ahead of me.

"We... Before we went on vacation, she kissed me."

"Who? Ashley?" he asked. Disbelief seeped through his voice.

"Yes," Jill whispered guiltily. With a red face, she looked down at her fidgeting fingers. "I'm sorry, I..." She didn't get to say anything else before tears welled up in her eyes and quietly streamed down her cheeks.

Dennis' hand slipped off my leg and he ran it through his blond curls. The spot where his hand had first been felt too cold. I could just about hear the gears rattling in his head. I had thought that when the truth came to light, the oppressive guilt would fall from my shoulders, but nothing was further from the truth. It only got worse. At this point I didn't even know what I was feeling.

"Dennis." I tried to get his attention. "Let me explain."

"Yeah, please! Because I don't understand a fuckin' thing." When he raised his face and sought my gaze, my heart broke. A glassy haze had appeared before his eyes, a tear escaped from the corner of his eye. But behind all of that I saw the anger that lurked, ready to escape at any moment.

I sighed. Jill should have kept her fucking mouth shut.

"Do you remember when I went home with Jill just after exams, before Lea came to get us and the five of us went out to do something?"

"Of course I remember that, that was barely a week ago."

"And do you also remember that we arrived fairly drunk?" I asked cautiously.

He squeezed his eyes to slits. "Yes?"

I looked cautiously around the group. "Maybe... Maybe it would be better if only the two of us talked in private? Not everyone..."

"No, I have nothing to hide from my friends. Tell me," he said forcefully.

I sighed deeply. "In Jill's room we had a drink in advance and we just got to talking. About our lives, the fact that high school is finally over, relationships...like normal girlfriends do. But then we started talking about our relationship and Jill asked if I missed us." A sob from Jill. I shut my eyes. It was so hard to get the words out. "Eventually we kissed. I don't know why; it was so stupid. Jill wanted to make sure we didn't have feelings for each other anymore."

"And did you?" Dennis asked with difficulty. From his tightened body, I could tell he was having trouble staying seated. I wouldn't want to listen to this either if I were him. Was it better if I said there were no feelings? Would he forgive me then? No, I couldn't lie now. I had better tell the whole truth.

I looked at my feet. "Yes, I still had feelings." A pressure appeared behind my eyes and they became moist. "Jill didn't."

A scream reverberated through the house as soon as I had spoken the words. My breath got stuck in my throat and I placed my hand on my heart, which felt like it was breaking into pieces. It seemed like it was a direct response to the scream that came from far away. Only then did the shock come. The scream had sounded heavy and masculine, almost like a roar. I turned to my friends, who all looked equally stricken.

"I wasn't the only one who heard that, was I?" Lea squeaked. She had hidden her face behind her reddish hair.

Kai shook his head. "No. There's probably someone walking around outside. I'm guessing drunk."

But it still really sounded like it was coming from inside. I must be going crazy...

"In the middle of a storm?" Jill looked at him incredulously.

He shrugged. "You never know what crazies are out there."

I played with my ring and slowly let the restrained tears run down my cheeks. The pressure in my heart that had just set in disappeared. Whether it was because of my sadness or the shock I didn't know, but Dennis snorted beside me.

"No, don't you dare cry. You don't have that right. And neither do you," he said after turning to Jill. He sprung up from the couch and staggered to his feet. "And after the kiss?"

The scream seemed to have been forgotten.

I glanced at Lea, who hung her head. "Lea caught us."

"And you didn't say anything to me either?" he shouted at Lea. "What is this? You all knew about it, and no one thought it was necessary to inform me?"

"Don't blame her," Jill interjected into the conversation. "Dennis, we made her promise not to say anything. Girl code."

"Fuck the girl code. This goes way beyond that! Kai, man, did you know?"

Kai shook his head bemusedly and looked at his girlfriend questioningly.

Dennis took a few deep breaths before turning to me. I almost cringed, not knowing what he was capable of. "We're going upstairs." He strode to the stairs and I walked behind him with buckling knees.

On the way up he balled his hands into fists and relaxed them again. He repeated this a few times. It was a nervous twitch I had seen more often. He led me to our room, at the very end of the hallway. He held the door open for me and once I was inside, he slammed it shut behind him with a loud bang. I was so startled that I put a hand over my mouth to muffle my scream.

Dennis fixed his deep blue eyes on me and rubbed his chin with his fingers. He pointed to the bed, gesturing me without words to sit on it.

I did as he asked of me. I tucked my hands under my legs so he couldn't see them twitching. It remained silent for far too long. Should I say something? What else could I do?

"You," he began. Then he pressed his lips together. "You..." He went through his hair with his hands, making it a tangled mess. In a flash, he turned and rammed his fist against the doorframe. It startled me. As Dennis shook his hand, whose knuckles were beginning to turn red, he leaned his head against the doorframe. His shoulders heaved up and down with heavy breathing in and out. "You made out with your ex." Sadness flashed through his eyes as he looked at me. "Why?" Dennis' shoulders hunched forward and his arms dangled limply alongside his body.

"I just told you that. I'm sorry."

"That's not what I asked. Why did you do it? You know my previous girlfriend cheated on me too, why would you do this?"

I buried my face in my hands. I had made a mistake. A big mistake. "It was a mistake," I said. "It should never have happened. We were drunk."

A scornful smile appeared on Dennis' face. "Oh, are you going to blame the booze now? I know you when you're drunk, Ashley. You may act weird, but you can think clearly enough. This was no 'accident'."

My head seemed to short-circuit. I couldn't think clearly anymore. I had to get myself out of this situation. "It was Jill! She suggested we try it."

"I don't give a damn about that. You agreed to it. And you said... You still have feelings for her. After all this time. Then why are you in a relationship with me at all!"

"Because I love you. I love you so much, Dennis. But feelings for a first love never really go away, I guess. You have no idea how sorry I am." Every time I looked at his face, my heart was further torn.

"Did it only happen that one time?"

"Yes," I spoke softly. But did that really matter anymore?

"Why don't I believe you?" Dennis came to stand in front of me and crossed his arms.

"Please believe me! I don't want to lose you," I begged. Hot tears streamed down my face. I really didn't want to lose him. He was the best thing that had ever happened to me. He had to believe me. It wasn't my fault. Jill wanted it so badly.

"I can't." Tears shone in his eyes. I watched him bite the inside of his lip, trying to hold back the tears. "No matter what the reason for your kiss was, you kissed. While you're both in relationships. You are each other's exes. You're my girlfriend, Jill is my best friend." His voice was shaking. "How could you guys do that?"

"We were drunk, it seemed so innocent..."

"I don't want to hear that excuse again. And I don't want to sleep in a bed with you anymore." He nodded in the direction of my suitcases. "Get your stuff and crawl under the covers with Jill."

My mouth fell open. He couldn't be serious. "I'm

not going to sleep with Jill!" I don't want to lose you, I wanted to say again. Please let me stay here, by your side, protected, I wanted to beg. But I couldn't get a sound over my lips anymore. With a drooping head I did what he asked of me. How could I ever make up for this?

Chapter 4

Ashley

My life had been destroyed. Drastically changed in less than ten minutes.

Dennis had ordered me to leave our bedroom. So there I was, alone in the hallway. There was no way I was going to sleep with Jill, that would only fuel his further suspicions. And not with Lea and Kai either, I couldn't do that to those two. But if I asked, they would say yes, they were like that. All my life I had something against being alone in a large space, so the slightly too small couch in the living room wasn't going to do it either. That left me with only one option.

Reluctantly, I opened the door to the junk room. I flicked on the light. I Immediately wrinkled my nose. We hadn't bothered to clean this room, something I now regretted. It smelled musty and my nose tingled from the dust. It was almost impossible to sleep among the filth. With the stuff that completely took up the space, I didn't even have the idea that this had ever been a bedroom. Against all the walls were closets, probably stuffed with all kinds of old junk. In front of those cabinets were pots, pans, chests full of photo albums and all sorts of other stuff. To my regret, I saw that the bathroom door from this room was barricaded by a huge, wooden cabinet. It was impossible for me to push that aside.

As I stood there by myself, I felt more alone than usual. My boyfriend had sent me away. I felt like everyone was angry with me, blaming me. But it wasn't just me who was in the wrong. Jill also had a part in the cheating. Hopefully, at this point, she was getting the same treatment I had just received.

Creaking footsteps in the hallway indicated that Dennis was on his way down. I bit my lower lip. He was recovering faster than I was. I wrinkled my nose again, wiped the dried tears from my cheeks, and studied the room. The only thing in the room that looked most like a bed was a cot. There was no mattress or blanket in sight.

"Huh, no way!" I whispered in frustration. And where was I supposed to get that stuff? There were no extra mattresses in the other bedrooms. I think this house still had an attic and a basement. Maybe I should go look there.

In the hallway, I searched the ceiling, looking for the string with which I could pull down the folding staircase that led to the attic. Within seconds I had found it, despite the fact that it was quite dark on the landing. I stood on my toes and was therefore just long enough to get hold of the string, but as soon as I got hold of it, the peculiar feeling came over me that I wouldn't find anything here. That I shouldn't go in there and that I was wasting my time by looking. I shook my shoulders in an attempt to get rid of the oppressive feeling.

I pulled and the piece of ceiling fell open, along

with a staircase that half unfolded itself. I jumped aside just in time to avoid getting hit by hit. Along with the stairs, a load of dust swirled down on me. It immediately began to tickle my nose and I sneezed twice. Obviously no one was cleaning up there at all.

"Mom, next time send a cleaning crew before sending your daughter and her friends to this house," I muttered to myself.

I looked at the hole above me. It was pitch black; I couldn't see what was in there. Bah, what if it was full of spiders or other creatures?

With difficulty I managed to unfold the loft ladder. This one didn't seem to be the sturdiest either. The wood showed several cracks and black spots, so I was careful when I climbed on it. As soon as I stuck my head through the hole and could look around the room, I noticed that there were no windows. The only light that seemed to reach the room was the light coming from the hallway.

With trembling arms, I hoisted myself up. "Bah, bah, bah," I whispered as the dust stuck to my hands. This was so not for me. I reluctantly crawled a bit further on all fours so that I was in the middle of the attic and took my phone out of my back pocket. I turned on the flashlight and shone it across the room. A shiver crept up my spine. I found the string for the light and pulled it, but nothing happened. After two tries, I realized the lamp was broken. Fine. I put my phone in the corner, so it illuminated the entire attic the best it could and began my search.

It was fairly empty here, compared to the junk

room downstairs. There were also several items, such as a crib, tools, and a closet, but most of it seemed to be broken. Useless. Why would anyone keep broken things? I didn't recognize them as belonging to my parents. The walls consisted of poorly mortared stone. The ceiling was made of wooden joists that were too far apart, so I could see the roof tiles on them. It was a miracle that the roof was still in one piece with that wind and rain outside. I laughed cynically. Yeah right, maybe all the cobwebs hanging here were holding everything together. At the sight of the webs, I felt as if countless spiders were itching over my body. After convincing myself that it wasn't real, I scanned the room. To my great relief, I saw a thin mattress in a dark corner and a few blankets sticking out of the closet. With a deep sigh, I stepped towards it. It would be a hassle to get all that down. A hassle I could have easily avoided if I hadn't... No, don't think about that. With swift movements I threw the blankets on the dusty mattress, which I then dragged to the hole in the wooden floor. And at that moment my gaze was drawn to the dark corner I had just come from.

The energy in the room changed. Where before it could not be felt, now it felt fraught. As if the air had grown thicker and was pressing down on me. On purpose. As if it wanted to claim my attention.

Out of the corner of my eye, I saw something white moving. God, no. Quickly I turned my head in that direction. There was nothing to see but dark shadows. Less than a second later, it appeared in the other corner of my eye. The laughter of a baby filled the room and the smell of roses and ginger invaded my nose. My breathing quickened and my heart pounded against my chest. Panic overtook me. I couldn't shake the awful feeling that someone was watching me.

A sigh on the back of my neck. Not a breeze that blew by, not a draft through the wall, but a concentrated exhalation into my neck. So cold it gave me goosebumps. Under my hair, I felt lips gently rubbing against my neck.

They whispered, "Ashley." It tasted my name. Spoke it again. As if it needed to get used to it. As if it wanted confirmation that it was me.

At random, I punched around me. But I hit nothing but air. And yet I felt it. I felt the eyes burning into my back, I felt the breath on my skin. Every cell in my body seemed to be telling me that someone was right behind me.

For a second I balled my hands into fists and squeezed my eyes tightly shut.

"Go away!" I shouted. As soon as I felt an entire palm pressing into my neck, I sprinted to my phone with great strides. My legs felt like pudding and everything seemed to be moving sluggishly. I didn't look back and just about jumped out of the hole. I could still think clearly enough to pull the mattress with me. There was no way I was going to go back because I had forgotten that darn mattress. I did everything in my power to get away as fast as possible. When I was back in the upstairs hallway, I planned to shine my phone's flashlight up into the black hole. But I changed my mind. If there was something there that could evoke such energy, I didn't want to see it. As quickly as I could, I folded up the stairs and closed the hatch. The silence on the landing was deafening.

"Guys!" I screamed. I sprinted to the stairs, ran down them. "Guys!"

They had obviously heard me, because when I sprinted into the living room, all heads were already turned in my direction.

"What?" Lea asked.

Words failed me. How could I tell this and at the same time avoid being made a fool of? I felt as if the energy from above was partly clinging to me. As if it didn't want to let go of me.

"You look like you've seen a ghost," Jill said, looking somewhat worried in my direction. My eyes slid to Dennis. He just sat there, not saying a word.

"I think I have."

"What?" Lea raised her eyebrows.

"In the attic. I was looking for a mattress to sleep on, in the junk room." My voice dropped. How much did Dennis tell already? Even though these were my best friends for years, it felt weird to share this information with them. Dennis looked away. I quickly recovered. "I went to look in the attic and I don't know exactly what it was, but it said my name and touched my neck. And that energy..." I shivered.

The four of them exchanged glances with each other. For a moment it seemed like they believed me, until Jill opened her mouth. "Ashley, are you being serious right now? Are you really going to make things up to get our, or Dennis', attention? You can't do that.

That's not how you should try to win someone over." She looked at me as if I had committed a major crime. A stabbing feeling shot through my heart.

"I'm telling the truth, why would I lie about this? There's something in the attic!"

Jill sighed. "Ash, please stop this charade, this whole situation is annoying enough."

"But..." Desperately, I searched for words to convince them. Surely they couldn't really think I was making this up to get pity? I had used that tactic in the past, but not now.

"Jill, what she said sounds too weird to be a lie. Why would she make up something so ridiculous when she could have said hundreds of other things that made sense?" Lea came to my rescue.

"Because she wants attention from Dennis, that's why." Jill turned her head away from me.

Dennis didn't say anything. Why should he?

"Okay, you guys don't believe me. Fine." Tears welled up in my eyes. "I thought we were friends. I'll wait until the same thing happens to you!"

Kai stood up and came to stand in front of me. As the tallest boy in the group, he towered high over me, the smallest girl. "Ash, I quite believe that you think you felt and heard that. But is there really no possibility that it could have been your imagination?"

I thought about the feeling I had before I opened the hatch. How dark it was up there, that I couldn't see my hand in front of my face at first. Then the sounds, my name, the lips and hand on my neck. My stomach turned.

"No, I can't possibly have imagined this." Right?

"Ghosts don't exist, Ash. There's bound to be some other explanation for whatever you've been experiencing," Kai said reassuringly. He rubbed my shoulders with his hands. I slapped them away.

"I didn't imagine it! There's nothing to explain this." My heart sank into my shoes. "Oh my god, what if there really is someone in this house? A drifter or something? Or a murderer!"

"There's no one in this house!" Jill stood up. "Otherwise we would have figured that out a long time ago. And now this business is done!" She was red-faced and looked like she might fly at my neck at any moment.

I bit my lower lip to hold back the tears. The group exchanged worried expressions with each other. They thought I was crazy. I could see it on their faces. "Never mind," I sighed defeatedly. I had no desire to be around people who questioned everything I said. Turning around, I gathered all my courage to walk up the stairs. Quickly I grabbed the mattress from the floor and dragged it to the junk room. No way I was going to look further into that dark hallway. With a thud, I dropped it on the wooden, dusty floor - which I was sure to clean later.

A box toppled over. Photographs ended up scattered across the floor. That too. With a deep sigh, I bent down to clean up the photos with trembling hands. While holding them, I couldn't help but look at them. The photos were so old that some of them had yellowed.

In the photo itself, I could see six people standing in front of a house. It looked like a family portrait. When I looked closer, I saw that they were standing in front of this house. The woman wore a simple dark gray long dress, with a white cloth in front, something that looked like a kitchen apron. The man wore a neat suit. The two boys also wore suits and the two girls wore the same kind of dress as their mother. All the women wore some kind of cap on their heads. I turned the piece of paper over and saw the year 1834 written on it. Stunned, I blew the air out of my lungs. That was really old. Could they take pictures back then? I didn't know and I didn't care. Everything I saw in the picture was of poor quality. Had this house been here so long? No wonder it looked like a ruin when perhaps almost nothing had been done to it since that time. Lost in thought, I rubbed my thumb over the woman's face.

It was kind of weird to see a picture from almost two hundred years ago that had been taken in the very place I was currently in. Kai and Lea would find this interesting, but since no one bothered to hear my story, I didn't bother showing it to them. Was it childish? Maybe. But normally we were there for each other. There was little of that now.

The wooden planks creaked under my feet as I began to tidy up the pictures. How I hated to be alone now. The fear was almost paralyzing. Despite everything, I was too stubborn to join my friends. I would have to do everything on my own.

Before I cleaned, I made the bed. It didn't feel particularly soft or comfortable, but I had to make do with it for the next few days. Maybe I could call my mother. I already had my phone in my hands when I realized there was no signal here, especially with this storm. I pulled my knees up to my chest. Tears welled up in my eyes. I wanted my mother.

Chapter 5

Kai

I looked at his face.

From the moment Dennis had walked back into the living room, the tension had been palpable. No one had said a word since his return. Before that, actually, no one had either. Jill had just been staring blankly into space and Lea and I didn't know what to say. My buddy had been betrayed by his own girlfriend and his best friend. I couldn't imagine how that must feel. Actually, I wanted to give him a heartfelt hug, but by the looks of it, now was not the right time. His eyes were red and his hands were shaking slightly. It seemed as if Dennis couldn't decide whether he was heartbroken or worked up.

I had put my arm around my girlfriend's shoulders and was pulling her closer to me. It seemed better to leave Dennis and Jill alone so they could talk freely. That thought got confirmed when Lea shifted back and forth a little uncomfortably.

I brought my mouth to her ear. Her hair tickled my lips. "Shall we go upstairs to give them space?"

Her big blue eyes fixed on me and immediately told me everything I needed to know. After two years, I knew that look. I smiled, pressed a kiss on her head and stood up with her.

"We're going upstairs," I announced as I was sent two questioning looks. My heart sank a little when Dennis didn't comment on that. Normally he would have said something along the lines of, "Don't make it too nice, huh," with a wink. The fact that he didn't do this made me worry about him and the situation. What would happen if we left them alone? No, I wasn't allowed to think that way. They were old enough to be able to discuss this.

On the way to the stairs, I put my hand on Lea's lower back. By the jolt that went through her body, I could feel what that did to her. She loved the small, simple touches, she was that romantic.

The creaking of the wooden stairs was drowned out by the wind roaring outside. It blew in through the crack that was in the wall next to the front door and the coolness stroked along my back.

Simultaneously with a dazzling flash, a huge bang thundered through the house that echoed through the mountains. Even the banister trembled from it. I wouldn't be surprised if the lightning had landed somewhere in the garden. The sudden noise and trembling caused Lea's foot to slip off the step. I managed to catch her just in time to prevent her from falling. Lea clasped her hands tightly around the banister.

"Ho, are you okay?" I asked after she was safely upright again. Lea rubbed her ankle for a moment, then nodded.

"Yes, thanks. It just seems to be getting worse out there," she continued as she looked through the window above the front door. Faster than before, we walked up the stairs. Upstairs we saw Ashley sitting in the junk room.

At first, she didn't seem to notice us, but after a while she looked up at us. Her eyes were bloodshot and thick bags hung beneath them. My lips softened to ask her how she was, but she shakily stood up and walked to the door.

"Not now," she said and she closed the door in front of us.

Lea took a deep breath and then slowly let the air out. "Let her be." She pulled me along to our room, which was at the far right end of the hallway. Because of all that was going on, I almost forgot that Lea knew about it, but hadn't said anything to me or Dennis.

Once we arrived in our room, I closed the door behind me. "Lea, why did you keep all this from me?" She caught on to the serious tone in my voice.

She sat down on the bed and gestured for me to take a seat next to her. The fact that she bit her bottom lip showed me that she felt guilty about it.

I took a seat next to her and rubbed her cheekbone with my thumb. Her cheeks were so soft and her eyes so deep blue that I could drown in them. Behind them, her thoughts seemed to be up for grabs, emotions flying through each other.

"Sorry," she sighed. She lowered her eyes. "I promised not to tell anyone. You know how I am with promises." Lea's loyalty to others was one of the reasons I liked her so much. You didn't often come across a person like that anymore.

"Some promises, like this one, you're better off breaking."

"I know, I know. Am I now a bad girlfriend because I didn't tell you? After all, I wasn't supposed to know either. Jill and Ashley had made me swear I wouldn't tell. That was our girl code. It's wrong what Jill and Ashley did, but still... I didn't know..."

I cut her off, otherwise she wouldn't stop rattling for a while. "It happened. It can't be reversed and now they have to face the consequences. There's nothing you can do about that part either. I'm just sorry you felt you couldn't share this with me."

"No, it's not that." She looked up at me with a cautious smile. "I feel like I can tell you everything, but in this case...well, I've actually already told you. I made a promise and I was so conflicted. I'm talking too much again, aren't I? I'm really sorry." Lea's voice trembled.

"I know that."

The corners of her mouth gently pulled up and formed a sad smile. "This was not what I imagined our vacation to be like. Almost everyone is arguing with each other and the weather is a disaster." She walked over to her bag and pulled out a notebook that lay on top. "I might as well throw away our entire schedule! Half of it we won't be able to do later if we even stay here, but probably everyone will want to go home as soon as the storm is over. And all the shopping I arranged, for nothing..."

I got up from the bed and stood in front of her. With my hands I cupped her face. She was so cute when she fussed and kept talking. I just had to make sure she didn't get caught up in it and panic.

"Lea, that's not true. Whatever happens, it will be okay." I hoped with all my heart that I could make this true. She deserved a peaceful vacation after a stressful graduation year. She had worked so hard and passed with flying colors. I eventually did too, although it was a little harder for me. I had to redo the eighth grade because I had failed too many subjects, and that's where I met Lea and my new friends. Sometimes I stayed up nights studying the material, but it almost never had the desired result. In fact, it had the opposite effect. I was so tired that I couldn't concentrate on the test. Fortunately, my mentor found this out and I had worked with him on it. I passed with my heels over the edge, but it was good enough for me.

Fingers stroking my back pulled me out of my thoughts. "Now you're overthinking," Lea chuckled. Her smile immediately awakened the jitters in my lower abdomen. Even after two years, this girl knew how to make my heart race. Was that what my mother meant by that 'you just knew'? I couldn't imagine ever cheating on her with another person, which made me wonder if Ashley really loved Dennis that much, especially since there were residual feelings for Jill.

I wrapped my arms tightly around her and pressed my nose into her neck. "I love you," I whispered.

"love you too."

My eyes slid to the window, behind which it colored dark blue and gray. Rain beat against the windows and partly because of that I couldn't see very far. Suddenly the sky was lit up by a lightning bolt that couldn't have been more than two hundred yards from here. My heart skipped a beat. There was someone standing in the back of the garden. She was looking straight at our window. Before I could see more, the outside world was once again enveloped in darkness. Immediately, a huge bang followed.

"I've never experienced it so bad," Lea whispered against my chest.

I slowly released her and walked to the window. "No, neither have I." With my hand over my eyes, I peered out. Had I seen it right? Someone was watching us. I took my phone out of my pocket and shone it through the window. Looking through the reflection in the glass, I could see a little more of the outside world, but not enough.

"What are you doing?" Lea asked, wrapping her arms around me from behind.

"I thought I saw someone standing in the garden."

Her arms stiffened around my body. "That's impossible. The gates are locked and apart from us there's no one here. Or do you think Ashley was right after all and that..."

"No, no. No worries. It was probably the light combined with the rain that made it seem that way."

"Indeed." She pressed a kiss to my neck. Lea was right. It was probably my imagination; we were the only ones here. There was a thought in my head that I could never imagine such a thing, but I didn't want to worry Lea any further. I laughed. And who was trying to reassure whom here?

Her lips caressed the side of my neck before she

pressed a kiss on it. I shuddered. She always knew how to find that sweet spot flawlessly. Her hands travelled to the bottom of my shirt and my skin began to tingle as she slid her fingers under it. My thoughts of what I thought I had seen immediately faded into the background. All I could think about was Lea.

I turned to her. I placed one hand on her lower back, then pulled her closer to me, and the other hand I placed behind her neck.

She looked at me expectantly. I melted at that look. I knew that if I kissed her, I would lose sight of reality. Lea would take me to another world where only the two of us existed. And I wanted that all so badly. Slowly I leaned forward until our lips were only a few inches apart. The closer she came, the faster my heart beat. Lea bridged the last bit and finally I felt her lips on mine. Tingles spread throughout my body. I thought again of how well she could seduce me and I didn't mind at all. She always knew exactly what I wanted, how to make the most of the moment. I could only dream of the time when I would give her the exact same feeling.

Her fingers tickled my neck and she pressed herself more firmly against me. She smiled against my lips after feeling her effect on me. Carefully I pushed her backwards, further and further, until her knees touched the edge of the bed and she fell onto the bed. I didn't immediately bend over her. Instead, I looked at her, at her face where there were a few freckles, the nose that she herself always thought was a little too big but I found charming, her deep blue eyes and red hair scattered around her. She leaned on her elbows and hoisted herself further up the bed. A smile lay around her pink full lips and with her index finger she gestured for me to come to her. I didn't have to think about that for a second. I climbed on top of her and kissed her full of devotion.

Chapter 6

Jill

They couldn't keep hurting each other or others.

I could have gone to my room when I realized I was left alone with Dennis in the living room, but I didn't. Neither did he. The two of us sat in the living room, each on our own couch. He was playing games on his phone and I was reading a book. Impatiently, I shook my foot. When was he going to say something? Or was I going to have to say something? I really didn't feel like staying in this uncomfortable situation. He needed to open his mouth. Even if it meant he was furious with me, at least that was something.

Sometimes I could feel his gaze burning into me. He probably thought I didn't realize it, that I was engrossed in my book. I couldn't concentrate on that, though, no matter how many times I tried. Words had been burning on my tongue for a long time.

"Say something, dude! Be mad at me or whatever, but I can't stand this silence."

He looked up, growled, and then continued his game. "I think you know very well that I'm angry with you, I don't have to say anything to let you know that." Even from here I could see that he was biting the inside of his lower lip.

"Dennis, let me at least explain my side of the

story. Let me..."

Now he locked his phone and tossed it aside. Quite aggressively he leaned forward and placed his elbows on his knees. "Are you really that stupid or secretly blonde?" The funny undertone that usually accompanied such comments was nowhere to be found.

I clapped my book shut. "What I did is unacceptable, I know, but what is this all about? Who do you think you are?"

"Oh, now I'm expressing my anger and it's not right again? And who am I? I'm someone whose girlfriend cheated on him with her ex!" He was running red. His clenched fists caused his veins to crawl under his skin. "For whom she also appears to have feelings!"

In contrast to his red face, all color drained from my face. The realization hit me like a bomb. At the time I had known that what I was proposing was not smart, but it meant nothing to me and that's why it seemed so innocent. "I... I'm sorry. I didn't mean for this to happen."

"Fuck, that doesn't matter! What matters is that you and Ashley are such airheads. What was your goal, man? What if the spark between you guys did happen? Would you have planned to break up with your girlfriend and live happily ever after together?"

"I... I don't know."

"Well, then. Man, I can barely look at you guys. Not only has Ashley betrayed me, but so have you. We've been friends for so long. What possessed you to kiss her? What possessed you? Fuck. I have so many emotions and questions, but I just don't know if I'm going to get honest answers to them."

"I don't think it's my place to answer them, I..."

"Not your place. Why not? Because Ashley's my girlfriend and you're not and so she gets to clean up this mess? No, Jill, that's not how it works. You caused this mess together, you're just as much a friend of mine. You have to answer for it too."

I gulped. There was a grain of truth in his reproach. I didn't want to throw away a friendship of years for something so stupid. That Dennis and Ashley had started dating after we had broken up... I hadn't gotten angry about that either. Friendship was above all else and therefore he was right.

"Fine. I'll answer your questions." I thought for a moment. I better word it right so this didn't escalate. "You've already heard most of this from Ashley." I explained again how we came to the moment we decided to kiss each other. The drink, we were alone, our relationship that came up in the conversation. "I was so stupid to suggest kissing. Believe me, I never in a million years would've thought Ashley still had feelings for me. For me, it was all over. She moved on with you and I got a new girlfriend. It wasn't smart, but since I knew I wouldn't have feelings for her, I figured it wasn't a big deal." I sighed and tried to gauge his reaction. He just sat there looking at his feet, so I continued. "And then Ashley said she felt more for me than intended. She was disappointed and angry when I said I didn't feel the same way anymore. You know Ashley, so you know what I mean when I say she hurled some pretty ugly words at my head. As you can imagine, I was not happy about that. Since we were all going on vacation a few days later, we decided to keep our mouths shut. We had made Lea promise to do the same. But apparently my anger was sitting pretty high. Maybe because of her words, maybe because of the fact that deep down I knew I had ruined everything. For myself." After the words left my mouth, I felt a little relieved. Still, the weight on my shoulders wouldn't completely disappear until Dennis...yeah, what exactly? Understood? He wouldn't.

He was quiet. Very quiet. He remained impassively seated in the same position. The only thing that moved was his chest moving up and down as he breathed. Finally he spoke. "Good to know that at least Ashley was telling the truth."

My hands were clammy with sweat and it didn't help that there were sweat spots under my armpits as well. I had wanted to avoid this situation at all costs.

"I can't believe Lea kept her mouth shut."

"Please don't be mad at her. It's not her fault. We asked her to keep quiet about it. She was probably torn between choosing to be loyal to you and tell you or being loyal to us and staying quiet." I shrugged. "That's how I know Lea."

"Yes, so do I. It's not fair of you guys to let her hang in there like that."

I fell back into the couch, against the railing, and crossed my arms. I hated it when someone else was right. Slowly I began to realize that in no scenario was I the 'good guy.' I was the bad guy. So was Ashley.

"I should mind my own business, but have you told your girlfriend yet?" Somehow he came across less angry.

I shrugged. Maybe it was best if I did. If everyone in our group knew, it was only fair that my own girlfriend was told the truth. Eventually. I would tell her as soon as possible, as soon as we got home from this flop vacation.

"One tip: tell her. Trust me. It sucks to know, but better than not finding out until much later."

"But you already know four days later."

"It's all about the principle. It hurts even more that Ashley and you wanted to keep this hidden." He looked at me penetratingly for an extended period of time, then he grabbed his phone again and continued with his game. That was the sign that the conversation was over.

After I found the right page, I started reading. Although I could not stay concentrated anymore.

Moments later, the silence was broken by Dennis' voice cutting through the silent room. "Do you hear that?"

"What?" Focusing on the sounds in the house, I slowly placed the bookmark between the pages. An unexpected sound reached my ears. "Is that...a baby?" I frowned. "No, it can't be. That must be the wind blowing through the cracks in the house." And yet it was unmistakably the sound of a baby crying.

Suddenly the temperature in the room changed and it became freezing cold. I slowly sat up and put the book down beside me. Goosebumps appeared on my arms, which I tried to remove by rubbing them with my hands. Something in this room didn't feel right anymore. First it was quiet and felt empty. Now it felt...full. I looked at the dark corners of the room where the light couldn't reach. Had I gone completely crazy? This was not like me.

"Oh, fuck!" Dennis called out so loudly that my head immediately flashed in his direction. "Fuck, fuck, fuck!"

I immediately jumped up and my heart rate skyrocketed. "What?"

He jumped up, dropped the phone from his hands and spun around on his axis. His chest was rising and falling so violently that I thought he was hyperventilating.

I looked around the room with him. "Why on earth are you scaring me like that?" I shouted.

"Fuck," he whispered, more to himself than to me. Sweat had spontaneously broken out on him. I saw a drop disappear from his hairline over his neck into his shirt. He was rooting through his hair with both hands, still looking around. "Did you hear that?"

"Other than what sounded like a baby crying, I didn't hear anything. All I heard after that was you."

"Fuck, man."

"Okay, now stop repeating the same word and tell me why you're acting like this!" Frustrated, I walked around the wooden side table to him and grabbed him by the arm. A jolt went through his body as my hand made contact with him.

"I... That voice... Fingers." He couldn't get more out of his throat. I recognized it. Panic that encompassed you so much that it squeezed your throat shut and you had to make every effort in the world to produce a sound at all.

Those few words immediately made me think of Ashley and the attic. I admonished him to calm down and then asked him again what made him so upset.

"It was bizarre, man. First I felt fingers on my neck...or a sigh...I don't know. And then I heard my name." He mimicked the voice. A whisper, weak and extended.

His words gave me the shivers.

"Are you kidding me?"

"No, I swear." He looked behind the couch again. "That wasn't you, was it?"

"No, I was on the couch the whole time." I cast a glance behind me, because the unpleasant feeling hadn't quite gone away.

"Did you see anyone?"

I shook my head. "If someone had walked in and out of the room, we would have noticed, I think." I clung to his arm and he clung to mine at the same time. This was very bizarre. At least, if I was to believe him. Dennis was known to everyone as a real prankster and I wouldn't be surprised if this was also one of his many games. And yet I believed him, for I felt the same fear.

Dennis exhaled slowly, as if doing breathing exercises. Only when I realized he was calming down did I let go of him.

"Could it be that the same thing happened to Ashley?" I watched him for a few seconds.

With big eyes he looked at me in dismay. "Ashley.

As I closed the clanging shutter this afternoon, someone walked into the room and put a hand on my back. I really thought it was Ashley, but...there was no one there at all when I turned around."

I wasn't scared, but my stomach turned. "This better not be a joke! Because that would be really disgusting of you."

"No, it really isn't!" He paused and looked at me as if he wanted confirmation from me that I believed him.

"I believe you." I swallowed a lump in my throat.

"Where are the others?" he asked suddenly.

For a moment I was confused, but I quickly answered his question. "I believe everyone is upstairs. Ashley didn't come down after your conversation and Kai and Lea went upstairs a little while ago. They're probably making out together." As if the universe decided to confirm my thoughts at this very moment, I heard the faint sound of a creaking bed. I deliberately made a gagging sound. "There you have your answer. Why do you want to know?"

Dennis shrugged. "No reason." Slowly he sank back on the couch. "Everything is okay. We'll stay in the living room. Together. Just the two of us. Not alone." He grabbed his phone again and tried to pretend that he was carefree continuing with his game.

I decided to follow his example and grabbed my book again. With my heart hammering against my chest, I tried to close myself off from my surroundings. Out of the corner of my eye, I saw movement near Dennis, but assuming it was one of our friends, I didn't look up.

Chapter 7

Lea

The knife pierced my lung, I felt it.

I fixed my hair in the bathroom mirror. Large tangles had formed in my curls. I saw that my mascara had smudged out. With my index fingers I rubbed under my eyes, removing the black stuff. In the reflection of the mirror I could see Kai lying on the bed. He was looking at me with a lopsided grin.

"What?" I asked, chuckling. I knew full well what he was going to answer, but this had become our thing.

"You look beautiful."

"So do you." He was lying half-naked on the bed and his athletic body from playing volleyball certainly didn't hurt my eyes. I bit my lower lip and quickly concentrated on getting myself decent again. Lost in thought, I acted on autopilot. A comb through my hair, a little more mascara.

Right behind me, a dark figure moved. Two firm hands grabbed my upper arms. I was so startled that I squeakily sucked in air. My first reaction was to pull my arm free and slam it backwards.

"Ouch, Lea!" Horrified, I turned around and looked straight into my boyfriend's pain-stricken face. He was rubbing his chest with his hand.

"Oh, sorry! I was so lost in thought that I didn't

even see that it was you. Everything was a big blur." I hurried to the sink and wet a washcloth with ice cold water. My heartbeat slowly went back to its normal rhythm. I pressed it to the spot where I had hit him with my elbow. Goosebumps appeared on his skin.

"I thought something like that. You're getting stronger, though. If you can't hit those balls hard in volleyball now, I don't know what will."

I ruffled my hand through his short frizzy hair. "I always have and you know it."

"Yeah, you bruise my ego every time our team has to practice with yours." I laughed out loud. We played volleyball at the same club and sometimes our coaches would organize practice matches. He was on the best boys team and my team was the best girls team. The matches were always very interesting, but usually we won.

"And after that, I always make it up to you." I stroked my lips along his, then pulled back. He chuckled, wrapping his arm around my lower back and pulling me against him. His soft lips touched mine and my heart pounded again, only this time for a different reason. With my fingers I stroked his equally soft skin. His delicious scent invaded my nose. After a few seconds, I detached myself from him.

"We'd better go downstairs, or they'll start suspecting things," I said.

Kai shrugged. "They will anyway. The bed creaked quite a bit."

My cheeks became warm. "Was it really that bad?"

"I think so." He laughed when I slapped my hand

in front of my mouth and said, "Look at this house, everything is old and creaks."

That was true. What did it even matter? The whole group knew we were sleeping together, so it wasn't that bad. I took one last look in the mirror while Kai put on his shirt and made my way downstairs.

"Ouch!" A fierce sting shot through my chest. I folded over and pressed my hand against the sore spot. It was the kind of pain I imagined when I saw someone on TV being stabbed with a knife.

"Lea?" Kai immediately stood beside me and supported me as he carried me to the bed. "What is it? Where are you hurting?" Step by step I came closer to the bed, and with each step I took, it stabbed again and more fiercely. I groaned. At last I sat bent over on the edge of the bed. The fierce sting continued to throb.

"I don't know what happened," I groaned.

"Let me see?"

I laboriously pulled my shirt up and pointed to the painful spot on my chest. The pain slowly ebbed away, but I was so startled that my fingers trembled from it.

"I don't see anything," he said. "Then it must be coming from inside. Surely not your heart? No, it's not in that spot. Something with your lungs?"

The pain almost completely subsided and slowly I stretched my body so that I was sitting upright again. I sighed in relief. What a relief. "Whatever it was, it's gone."

"I'm not comfortable with it. Just take it easy and get yourself checked out by the doctor." His concerned brown eyes studied me.

I smiled and framed his face with my hands. "Kai, it's all right again. Sometimes you have these random pains in your body. It doesn't always have to mean something." A little voice in the back of my head said, *Yes it does, listen, feel.*

What? Confused, I shook my head. Wow, maybe that sting had done some damage after all. Maybe I needed to see a doctor after all.

Kai frowned worriedly, but then stood up. "Are you able to walk downstairs?"

I nodded and together we walked down the stairs.

Ashley was also in the living room this time. Dennis, Jill and she were rather quiet, but not hostile. Was that progress?

"Ashley, what are you doing here?" Kai asked. "I didn't hear you go downstairs."

"Yes, your bed was disturbing my peace." With a half-hearted smile, she rolled her eyes. Maybe it wasn't so smart to flaunt our relationship when hers had just broken up. No, Lea, I told myself sternly. This was very upsetting for her, but my relationship didn't have to suffer for that.

Ashley brought her fingers to her other hand. She frowned before looking down at her hand. "No, no, no! Where is it?" she jumped up from the couch and commanded Jill and Dennis to do the same. Cautiously, not understanding what was going on, they stood up. Ashley frantically grabbed the pillows that were on the couch and threw them on the floor. With her hand, she groped the entire piece of furniture. Even the seat cushions were pulled off. When she found nothing there, she searched further in the living room without tidying up the couch again.

"Um, Ashley? What did you lose?" I asked. I bent down to grab a pillow and put it back on the couch.

"My ring! You know, the one I got from Grandma before she died. I never take it off." Panic was written on her face.

"And now it's gone?"

"Yes, you idiot!" she yelled at me. "Why else am I standing here looking for it?" She was breathing hurriedly and her hands were shaking so badly she wouldn't even be able to hold a glass without dropping it.

"When are you sure you last saw it?" Kai asked.

Ashley stopped moving and thought. "Just now, in the junk room. Or no...this morning. Yes, it was definitely on my finger in the car. Then I was still playing with it. And when I looked out the window right before Dennis and Jill grabbed your phone as a joke."

"Okay, and that was the last time?" I asked, just to be sure.

"I've had that ring for so long, I don't even notice I'm wearing it anymore. But that was the only time I became aware that I was wearing that ring." An agonized sound escaped from her throat. "Oh, no. I can't lose another thing this vacation!"

Poor girl. I looked at the person she was referring to. Dennis' lips were pressed together into a thin line.

"Really, have none of you seen my ring?" Her bottom lip quivered.

I dug into my mind, but I couldn't remember seeing her ring anywhere. "No," I replied regretfully, while everyone else shook their heads as well. I made an attempt to quiet her by putting my hand on her shoulder, but she shook me off and continued to pace through the living room.

"Someone must have that thing! It can't just have disappeared. It's always just a little too tight, so it can't have slipped off my finger either." She continued searching around the couches, pushing aside tables and chairs and even lifting the rug. "Please, one of you must have it. Did someone take it off my finger?"

What in heaven's name? We would never keep something so precious from her. Not even Dennis in this case.

"Ash, wouldn't you have noticed if we had taken it off your fingers?" Jill asked.

"Not if my mind was off it. Maybe we were joking and fooling around so I didn't notice."

"Ashley, no, of course not," Kai tried.

"Of course not, just like this morning with Lea's phone surely?" she looked at Jill and Dennis. Her eyes were spitting fire.

Dennis swallowed and crossed his arms. "I don't want anything to do with you anymore, do you really think I would take that stupid ring away from you?"

"Stupid?! Look, I may have cheated on you, but that doesn't mean you suddenly have to act like a complete asshole!" she shouted as loudly as she could. "I'm going to check your bags. All of yours!" Ashley ran in the direction of the stairs.

She was thinking irrationally. We had no reason or opportunity to steal that ring from her.

"Ash! You can't just go through everyone's personal stuff, have you gone completely crazy?" Jill stomped after her. "Privacy!"

"If you guys have nothing to hide, you'll let me look," I heard her yell halfway up the stairs.

She had lost it. Of course I understood how much that ring meant to her and Ashley always acted a little over the top, but I had never experienced this. In the living room, we couldn't see what was happening on the stairs, let alone the second floor. All I could hear was a lot of stumbling and screaming from Ashley and Jill.

Less than a minute later, Ashley was running downstairs with Jill at her heels. Ashley's cheeks were wet and red with tears and with anger, which made it clear that she hadn't found her ring among our things.

As she stood in the living room, looking around hysterically, her gaze suddenly fixed on the window.

"Didn't I say so!" she yelled, pointing at it. "We are not alone in this house. She has my ring!"

Before I could even look in the direction she was pointing, I heard her walk away behind me, then fumble at the coat rack. It only took a split second, but I swore I saw someone standing in the garden.

"Has she gone mad?" hissed Jill. "Wait!" she called out to Ashley.

For a moment she appeared back around the corner. "That ring is the only thing I have from my grandmother, okay! I just can't lose that one."

Kai walked with firm steps towards the hallway. "Ash, act normal!"

I heard no reply, instead the front door opened and closed again. "Oh, no. Don't tell me she went out there by herself in this storm, with an unknown person standing in the yard!" Instinctively, I ran to the hallway and I grabbed my coat and phone to use as a flashlight. I left the umbrella I had brought just to be safe; it was too windy for that.

Kai grabbed my arm. "Lea, what are you doing?"

"What do you think? I'm going after her. She needs to go back inside."

He also grabbed a coat and a flashlight. "Then I'll go with you. I won't let you go out by yourself."

Dennis and Jill sighed simultaneously. "We'll go too."

I smiled. That they were willing to put aside their feelings toward Ashley to help her – and us – meant a lot to me. And to the band of the group.

Kai opened the door and immediately the wind and rain hit my face. I brought my hand up to protect my face. It was blowing so hard that I was forced to take a step backwards. With the help of Dennis, who was standing behind me, I walked forward, out of the house. Then he supported Jill and Kai put his arm around me. Because of the raindrops that were streaking my face, I couldn't see a thing.

"Ashley!" I called out, but I couldn't see her anywhere. "Ashley, where are you?" Ahead of us, a faint shout sounded. That had to be her. We got closer and I could see her better and better.

"What are you guys doing here?"

"Stopping you, of course. You shouldn't go out alone in this weather," Kai replied, a little irritated. Ashley wanted to say more but decided against it anyway.

"Get inside!" I called out, trying to raise my voice above the wind.

"No, I'm not leaving until I find my ring. You search here and maybe on the ground too. I'm going after that woman!" There was so much conviction in her voice that I acquiesced. Just to be sure, I looked around carefully. Besides Ashley, was I the only one who had seen someone standing in the garden? It seemed so, as the others exchanged confused expressions with each other.

"Woman?" Kai yelled after her. "Wait, I'll go after her, you guys stay here." And away he went.

I sighed deeply and grabbed my phone, which I protected with my arms, and turned on the flashlight function. The lights from our flashlights chased the darkness away a bit. I shone over the ground, but saw nothing but grass, twigs, leaves, and sand. Because a phone's flashlight didn't shine wide and thus always illuminated a small area, it was extra difficult to see around me properly. I was afraid of missing an area, so I went over the same patch several times. Meanwhile, I was getting soaked by the rain.

I was so focused on searching that I didn't notice at first that I could barely see the ground anymore. I blinked, thinking there was a raindrop in my eyes that was blurring my vision. It didn't help. Slowly it dawned on me that the so-called haze I was seeing was moving, and it wasn't my eyes. White fog had gathered around my feet, obstructing my view of the earth. It was pressing closer and closer together, whiter and whiter.

I looked up at the others, but I could barely see them anymore. Only a few vague outlines were visible. I think I had strayed from the group. I shone in their direction. "Kai?"

"Lea, is that you?" I heard him ask.

"Yes." As fast as I could I ran towards them. I almost bumped into my boyfriend. I hadn't seen him standing there through the dense fog.

A hand grabbed my arm and I immediately felt it was Ashley. "Is everyone standing here?" she asked. She shivered.

"I think we're all here," Kai confirmed.

"But..." began Jill. I saw her finger go past my face and point at something in front of us. "If we're all here...who's that?"

"Dennis, this isn't funny!" Ashley cried, who had apparently already seen what Jill was referring to.

"What? I'm standing behind you guys!"

"Then I think we've found the woman," Ashley said with a trembling voice.

Everyone really was standing here.

I followed Jill's finger. Through the dense fog, I had to try my best to see something. What looked like the outline of a human being emerged in the fog, but it was hard to make out. I thought I vaguely saw a dress and long hair blowing in the wind. My breath caught in my throat and a shiver ran from the tip of my toes to the top of my crown. Or was it a tree after all?

It became deathly quiet. All I could hear was everyone's breathing. The sound of wind and rain faded into the background.

"Am I hearing a baby again?" whispered Jill.

Dennis cleared his throat. "He's laughing."

A pleasant scent of roses and ginger tea spread into the air.

"I think I saw her standing in the garden earlier too." Kai's voice cut through the air like a razor-sharp knife through meat.

"What, why didn't you say anything to me? And is that really a woman? I can barely see it."

"Because I didn't want to worry you. It looks like a woman, but I'm not sure."

"Shh," Jill hissed.

"We're going inside," Kai whispered more softly now.

"Are you crazy?" Ashley's voice was shaking so badly I could hardly understand her. "We have to go right past her."

Apparently they were convinced that someone was standing there, but I wasn't.

Jill gulped. "I wonder if it's a person at all."

Aha, see?

"What?" escaped shakily from Ashley's mouth.

"It's a statue," Jill tried to reassure us. Or herself.

Just then, a bolt of lightning struck a tree dozens of feet away, illuminating the surrounding area for a moment. I stared straight into two bright white eyes. The figure's hair was wet and blowing wispy around her face. Her mouth hung open. Then it got dark again and I couldn't see her clearly anymore.

I let out a groan and squeezed my eyes tightly shut. Okay, that looked way too real for a statue.

"That wasn't a fucking statue!" Dennis cried out.

Kai's familiar voice sounded right behind me. "We'll walk right past it. Don't look, just go in."

No one said anything, but it was clear that everyone would do as he said.

"On three," he said. I grabbed his hand and moved closer to him. "One, two, three." We got moving.

With quick but careful steps, so as not to trip over the earth and branches we could no longer see, we walked toward the house. I squeezed my eyes to slits, trying not to look at the woman's shadow in the fog. I heard the footsteps of Ashley, Dennis and Jill behind me. Hurried breaths filled the air. Finally, the door to the house came into view. Jill was the one who made a final sprint and smashed open the door, running into the house and gesturing for us to come as quickly as possible. I didn't think twice about that. Kai apparently didn't either, because he pulled me in with him. When Dennis and Ashley were also inside, Kai slammed the door shut behind us.

Chapter 8

Dennis

Arriving in their bedroom, I saw what havoc had been wreaked. Their bedspread had been ripped off their beds and all kinds of toys were scattered all over the room.

We hadn't been inside for a second when a thunderclap echoed through the mountains again. A flash of light illuminated my friends' faces. Water droplets dripped from our hair, clothes and bodies onto the ground. A small puddle of water had formed. Kai was still leaning against the door, as if trying to hold something back. Lea stood close to him with her arms wrapped around herself. My eyes shot to Ashley. The first thing I saw was her hands shaking, but I quickly came to the conclusion that she was shivering from head to toe. I'm sure that wasn't because of the cold. What on earth had we just seen? I didn't want to believe it. We were the only damn people on this property. Another flash of light. All the lights went out.

I held my breath and heard Ashley make a squeaking noise. It was eerily dark without the lights of this house. It took a while for my eyes to adjust. I watched as Jill rubbed Ashley's back comfortingly.

"The fuses probably blew," Lea said. Immediately the house was enveloped in light again, eliciting a squeal from her.

"I'll light the fireplace to warm us up," Jill suggested. She took off her own coat, and Ashley's. Lea, Kai and I followed her lead. To my surprise, everyone's coat was fairly rainproof, so our upper bodies weren't as soaked.

"Then I'll get some hot drinks ready," Kai said. While Kai walked to the kitchen, the rest of us decided to sit in the living room.

"Where's the wood?" I asked Jill. My lips felt numb as I spoke. As if they had become quite hypothermic, but it wasn't cold enough for that, despite the rain.

"Next to the fireplace." On autopilot, Jill reached for the wood and placed it in the fireplace. The sharp remarks I had expected from her did not come. Jill looked stoically ahead as she worked.

"My ring. It's gone," Ashley whispered defeatedly. She sat on the couch behind me. A tear rolled down her already wet face. Her blonde hair was stuck to her face and her makeup was smeared.

A stab went through my heart and I had to swallow away a lump in my throat. I took a seat next to her and put a hand on her leg. As angry as I was with her, I knew how much that ring meant to her and I regretted my remark earlier. "The weather was way too bad to see anything, we'll look again when the storm has passed."

Ashley nodded absently, as if my words didn't really get through to her. She looked down at her hand, at the bare finger. We would find the ring; I was sure of that. After all, there was no way it could just be gone.

I was distracted by the warmth that stroked my face. I looked up and saw the fire in the fireplace burning. The shadows it cast on the walls of the house suddenly brought an ominous glow with it. As if it wanted to say that the event of just now was only the beginning, as if it wanted to reinforce my anxious feelings. The dark spots that were on the wood seemed to take the shape of faces with the flickering of the flames. I averted my gaze from the walls.

"Indeed, Ash," Lea said, "we'll find it."

Ashley shrugged. "Thanks, Lea." She smiled faintly.

Jill stood up in front of the fireplace and joined us. "Well, it's burning." Her voice sounded so much softer than usual. The fierceness was gone.

"Shouldn't one of us check to see if that woman is still outside?" Lea asked. "Because technically she's on our property and that's illegal."

"Hey, hello, do you think we're going out there now? That's way too dangerous!" Ashley shouted panicked.

Oh right, and who was the one who ran out in a hurry just now?

I nodded. "She's right. Kai just now said that he had seen her earlier today too, so she's probably been here for a while. We'd better not go out and keep everything locked up tight." Something was gnawing at me, but I couldn't put my finger on it. Outside, it had seemed like...she didn't really exist. She was there, but then again she wasn't. I could see through her, she looked ridiculous and who was standing outside in this weather? I didn't trust it. This wasn't funny anymore, man.

Footsteps in the hallway came this way. Kai walked into the room with a tray full of mugs from which steam was rising. "Here." He handed each one of us a mug.

My hands trembled as I took my mug. With two hands I clasped the thing and pressed it to my leg, welcoming the warmth that came from it. Cautiously, I took a sip of the hot chocolate milk. A little too warm, but my body was grateful for it.

"Let's think rationally," Kai said, sinking onto the couch next to Lea and handing her a mug. "We're all startled, but we couldn't see very well outside because of the rain, wind and fog, so we don't know if we really saw what we thought we saw."

Jill was the first to jump up and object. "How can you say that? You saw it with your own eyes! There was someone standing in the garden."

Oh man, had there really been someone walking on this property, around this house, all day? Was she watching us? The fact that she was probably still standing there now made the situation more grim. Who knows, maybe she was going to keep sneaking around here until we were gone. No, that was impossible, wasn't it? There was no one standing in the yard. It was probably a statue and the storm and atmosphere had probably made me imagine strange things. When we got here it was raining hard too and I had to confess that I hadn't taken the time to look around properly. At least, that's what I told myself.

"The fog was thick. Maybe it was a...statue...or a rake..." I tried. "Who knows, maybe this place has a gardener."

Jill looked at me as if I said that two plus two was six. "You don't really think anyone is updating the garden in this weather, do you? Then a statue sounds most believable."

Kai agreed. "It was probably a statue. What else could it be?"

"You know what?" Ashley's voice sounded much firmer than before. "I hope you all experience something tonight that cannot be explained and scares the hell out of you. Then you'll speak differently about the matter. Something weird already happened to me, remember? Didn't it happen to you too, Dennis? Why are we sitting here trying to rule out the logical?"

"And what do you think the logical is?" Jill asked.

"We're not alone in this house. There's something going on here."

No, she shouldn't have said that. I didn't want to face it. Still, my thoughts went back to less than an hour ago. I remembered the icy fingers on my neck, breath hitting my ear as a low, male voice whispered my name. The crying of a baby... So what did all that mean? I didn't have an explanation, but what Ashley suggested was completely impossible. I kept my mouth shut, afraid of escalating this situation and getting into a heated argument with Jill and Ashley.

Suddenly I seemed to notice all the noises around me, but the things that startled me turned out to be false alarms. The movement in the corner of the room was from the lamp, the whistling in the hallway was the wind blowing through the crack under the door, and the creaking from upstairs were small animals running on the roof. Everything had a logical explanation...except for that translucent figure.

Lea looked around. "Whatever we saw, it is outside." Her always pale skin seemed even whiter now. Even in this state, she was trying to reassure Ashley. But she was right. If anything, it couldn't get in, because we had the doors and windows tightly closed.

"But who knows, it might still get in." Ashley kept rubbing her hand over her thigh, as if she had constant sweaty hands that she couldn't get rid of.

I took a few sips of the chocolate milk that had cooled a bit by now. "Is anyone hungry?" I didn't realize what a stupid question that was until the words had already left my mouth. Could anyone get a bite down their throat? Still, everyone but Ashley nodded. It took me a moment to realize that everyone was looking at me expectantly. Oh, of course. I had suggested it, so I could go get something to eat. "I'll make something."

I placed my mug on the table and walked to the kitchen. Why was it so much darker in here than in the living room? The lights were on. Besides, why was the whole area around the house so much darker than the world outside? It gave me a grim feeling. Claustrophobic, you could almost say. Even with the worst storms in the Netherlands I had never seen it so dark. With tense shoulders, I pulled a tray of plates from the cupboard. I rummaged through the refrigerator, looking for something to snack on. In the end I went for some toast with spreads and a bowl of chips.

Just as I was about to pick up the tray and walk to the living room, a cold shiver ran down my spine. The hairs on the back of my neck stood up. An ominous feeling took hold of me.

A sound that I would have preferred not to hear again penetrated my ears. Again that crying baby. Man, what was that all about? A gust of wind swept along behind my back and seemed to briefly pull at my shirt. As if stiffened, I clung to the countertop. Cold sweat slid down my back. I felt that someone was standing behind me. Eyes burned into my back. I gathered all my courage and slowly turned my head in that direction. Just as I turned my whole body, a vase flew straight at me. I reacted just before the object could hit me and dove down. The vase burst above my head against the kitchen cabinet. Glass pieces fell down my neck and slid into my shirt. I breathed in so sharply that I produced a squeaking sound. In the corner of my eye, I saw a dark apparition disappear.

"Dennis?" Lea came running around the corner. "Dennis!" She rushed over to me. The shards of glass crackled under her shoes. "What happened?"

Everyone else came into the kitchen as well.

"What is this supposed to be?" Jill asked.

Kai grabbed my arm and hoisted me up. "Dude, are you okay?"

I leaned against the counter and felt the blood drain from my face. As I tried to catch my breath, I made an attempt to get my thoughts in order. What had just happened? After a while I regained my voice. Gasping, I said, "I...felt someone standing behind me and...when I turned around, this...vase suddenly came at me." They looked at the shards in my shirt.

"Didn't you just throw that yourself?" Jill asked. She lifted my shirt and shook it. Several shards of glass clattered to the ground. She tried to pluck the rest carefully from the fabric.

"No, that thing was standing there. I'm very sure of that," I replied. I pointed to the little table further down the hall. There was no way I could touch that from here myself.

Lea agreed. "There was indeed a vase there."

"Are you hurt?" Ashley asked, referring to the shards that had hit me.

"I don't think so." I inspected what I could see and Jill looked down my back.

"Other than three scratches there's nothing serious, they're not even bleeding," she said when she was done. I had been lucky. This could have ended much worse.

"Then why did you throw that vase?" Ashley exclaimed. "Who knows, maybe it was an antique!"

"What?" Completely taken off guard, I stared at her.

"Those jokes of yours go way too far! We just went through something scary, where no one wants to believe me, and now you think it's funny to make the situation worse?" Ashley was running red. Her knuckles turned white as she clenched her hands tightly into fists. "You always pull pranks like this, but this is not the time!"

"Ash, I didn't throw that vase."

She laughed cynically. "Oh, right. Then who did? I believe we saw someone in the garden, I think I'm the only one who did, but I'm pretty sure there was no one in this house who could have thrown the vase. No one but you."

Her statement sounded so convincing that even I began to doubt myself. The others looked thoughtfully.

"I swear it wasn't me. My jokes never go that far! Breaking something and putting myself in danger in the process? Come on. After what just happened, the fun is gone." I looked at them desperately. "Guys?"

"Sorry, Dennis," Lea said, "but Ashley's right. This is going too far." I could read the regret on her face, but that didn't take away from the fact that she didn't believe me.

Kai gave me an encouraging slap on the shoulder as the girls walked back to the living room. "I know you want to keep the situation light-hearted, but this is not the way." He smiled at me with lips pressed together. "I'll take the food, but you have got to clean this up. Sorry, dude, it's your own mess. We'll save some for you."

"Man, I just don't get why you guys won't believe me after what happened outside."

Kai frowned. "You didn't believe in that either, did you?"

"I... Maybe. When I was alone with Jill something happened that I still can't quite explain and with what happened just now... I didn't want to believe it, but I think there's something really weird going on in this house."

Chapter 9

Ashley

No, I couldn't believe that. With a gaping mouth I stared at the scene.

I looked at Dennis angrily as he took his seat on the couch. He had spent the past fifteen minutes cleaning up the shards, which he said he had not caused himself. You didn't have to be a genius to know that was a lie. Dennis was the type to keep a situation light-hearted by playing pranks, but breaking something went too far. And then also claiming he hadn't done it? Pretending someone was in the house to scare us? Or...was he telling the truth after all? No, of course no one had come in, we were here the whole time and didn't hear or see anyone. But what if someone had snuck into the house while we were outside? I squeezed my forearm fiercely to distract myself from this ridiculous thought.

The panic and hysteria I had felt earlier faded and I only felt tired. Defeated, I rubbed my hands over the dried raindrops on my cheeks. My eyes fell on the black spots on my fingers. I sighed deeply. Now I probably looked like a panda too. Actually, I wanted to go upstairs to get that stuff off my face, but after what had just happened, I didn't dare go alone. I thought about earlier today in the attic, when I was there looking for a new mattress. The only person who would believe me and would want to help me was Lea. I bit my lip as I searched for the right words.

I cleared my throat. "Lea?"

She turned her head in my direction. Apparently I had interrupted her conversation with Kai. "Yes?" She studied me with her big eyes.

"Do you want to go upstairs with me?"

Lea raised an eyebrow. "Um, okay. Why?"

I shrugged. "I want to clean my face."

At that she nodded understandingly. Still, I noticed from the way she slowly stood up and glanced at Kai that she had doubts. Was she that scared too? That made me feel a lot less alone. Together we walked upstairs. With every step I took the cells in my body seemed to be screaming at me to get out of here. I persevered. Surely this was my parents' family home, I was not going to be chased out of here! My dejection had turned to anger. And I was going to get my damn ring back!

On our way to the bathroom I shared with Dennis, we passed the entrance to the attic. A cold shiver ran down my spine. I forced myself to look straight ahead.

"Ashley, I didn't want to ask downstairs, but why did I have to go with you?"

I bit the inside of my cheek. "Because I'm too scared to go alone. What if there really is someone walking around this compound?"

Lea rubbed her arms with her hands. "Yes, I'm afraid of that too, but I try to not let it drive me crazy. What are the chances of someone deciding to sneak into our house in this weather? Maybe we're all just tired from the trip." Doubt echoed through her voice. That didn't exactly convince me. "Is it all right if I just change and freshen up in my own room?"

I nodded, though I would have preferred to shout no. Lea headed for her room. I turned around and entered the junk room, where I would be sleeping from now on. With my toiletry bag, I walked through the hallway to the bathroom, because the door entering the bathroom in the junk room was blocked by a huge closet with all kinds of stuff in front of it.

I was shocked when I looked in the mirror. The mascara had run all over my cheeks to my chin. The rubbing had caused it to smear all over. I sighed wearily and took the items out of my toiletry bag. I lined up my grooming products. Then I wouldn't have to do that again.

I turned the faucet on and made sure the water wasn't too hot. I had heard that cold water was better for cleansing your skin than hot water. The fresh water I splashed on my face gave me a boost. With my eyes closed, I hunched over the sink. I smelled a wonderful scent. Roses and something I couldn't place. I frowned. I hadn't added soap or anything to the water, had I? It must have been Lea spraying some perfume or something.

The piercing laughter of a baby filled the room. I stiffened. I had heard that laugh before. I felt my heart beat everywhere in my body. Still, I was hunched over the sink, with my face soaking wet and my eyes closed so as not to get water in them. The laughter grew louder, as if moving through the bathroom, closer and closer in my direction. Slowly, I reached for my towel. I pressed it against my face so I could finally open my eyes. The first thing I saw was the mirror. It only lasted a split second, but it was enough to almost make me fall on my knees. There was someone standing behind me in the room. My knees went weak and I held myself up by gripping the sink. My heart was pounding in my throat and in reflex I looked behind me. No one. Just an empty space. After thoroughly scanning the bathroom with my eyes, I took a somewhat relieved breath. My head was playing a nasty game with me. One time I thought I experienced something and my brain fabricated all kinds of weird pictures. As I leaned against the sink and stood panting, I laughed softly to myself.

I turned around so I could continue my facial routine and looked straight into a pair of bright white eyes in the mirror. An additional face was right next to mine. Instead of my blonde hair, she had long black hair. Instead of my small, sturdy figure, she looked like a grim thin skeleton. And that face... The cheeks had sunken in so far that the cheekbones stuck out. She smiled. There was something sinister about her gaze.

I flinched to the side, away from her. She was really there. This was not my imagination. "Lea!" I screamed. I didn't get an immediate answer. "Lea!" I heard footsteps in the hallway rushing toward me. I turned to the door the moment her footsteps stopped there. When Lea opened the door and I turned to the mirror, the woman was gone. My gaze shot in all directions. Where had she gone?

Lea stormed into the bathroom. "What is it?" She had her arms outstretched before I reached her. I buried my face in her neck. My hands were shaking uncontrollably. Warm tears rolled down my cheeks. Instantly, I felt a lot safer.

"Ashley, calm down," she soothed. "What happened?" She pushed me away from her a little so she could look at me. Lea studies me as if she wanted to read the story off my face.

I avoided her eyes. She wouldn't believe me. I didn't even believe myself. Not even a few seconds ago I thought it was my own imagination. "I saw... I don't know..." rolled over my lips with difficulty. "I saw someone, or something, in the mirror." My voice was shaking so badly I had to struggle to understand myself. I pointed to the spot in the bathroom where I had seen her standing. "What is going on with this house?" I shouted in frustration.

Lea looked over my shoulder. "I don't see anything." Reassuring words slipped across her lips, but they didn't mean anything to me.

"I want to get out of here," I squeaked. There wasn't a hair on my head that thought of looking again.

She nodded and we left the bathroom. Lea closed the door behind us. On the way downstairs she asked, "What exactly did you see? Wasn't it just your own reflection?"

I shook my head frantically. "No, I saw my face as well as someone else's. She was standing behind me." Shivers immediately ran down my spine at the thought. It looked so evil and fragile at the same time. Another image took its place. "Call me crazy, but she looked ridiculously similar to the person we saw outside." The blood drained from my face. "Oh my god, Lea, she's inside, she's really inside! Dennis was telling the truth!"

"Ash, are you sure your brain isn't playing tricks on you?"

"I've never been so sure of anything! I couldn't have made this up even if I wanted to."

Lea's facial expression changed. It no longer appeared as incredulous as it had a few seconds ago. The fear I saw behind her attempt at a reassuring smile squeezed my throat. "I believe you," she said. We walked into the living room. Our friends stared at us. I guess it wasn't hard to see that something was going on. I still felt like I looked like crap.

Dennis was the first to get up and stand in front of me. He didn't have to say anything. He knew something had happened. I couldn't manage to open my mouth, so Lea told everything she knew. The others listened breathlessly.

"This is no longer a coincidence," Dennis said. He turned to the rest. "You won't believe I didn't throw that vase, but meanwhile Ashley and I have both been through something twice. And just now, outside, how are you going to explain that? I didn't want to believe it at first either, but there's something weird going on. There's no statue outside, nobody goes outside during a storm like that. So what option is left?"

Lea took a sharp breath. "You don't mean..."

"Ghosts. Demons. Whatever they are."

"Come on, don't be ridiculous!" Jill stood up.

"Those don't exist. There's no way someone isn't pulling a prank on us. Did you secretly invite some of your friends over, Dennis?"

A frustrated tear escaped the corner of my eye. "Really, Jill? You think we're just making this up?"

"I believe you believe you saw something, but that doesn't mean the place is haunted."

Lea took a step forward. "And what do you think it is?"

"A TV show, the boys playing a prank, I don't know. But what you're suggesting doesn't exist. Has anyone searched for cameras yet?"

"Talking about logical explanations," Dennis growled. "No, there are no cameras."

"Kai?" Lea asked. "What do you think?"

He got up and walked over to his friend. Hopefully Kai believed me, because when he was sure of something, the rest quickly followed. "I don't know what's going on here, I just know that it's not normal for so many of us to be startled. But other than that, I agree with Jill. I don't believe in ghosts."

Chapter 10

Kai

My little girl was taking small, shock like breaths, blood seeping from her mouth because of the internal injuries.

"Do you really not believe Ashley?" Lea asked. We were standing in the kitchen preparing dinner. After tempers had calmed, everyone had sat down in the living room. Dennis was playing a game on his phone and Jill had grabbed a book. Ashley was lying on a couch by herself, having announced that she was tired. When Dennis' stomach growled, we decided it was time for dinner.

"As Jill said, I do believe she thinks she saw that. Why?"

"I mean, well, she seemed pretty upset to me. Even Ashley isn't that good of an actress." She turned the baked potatoes over so she could get them well fried on all sides.

"I would be too if my brain presented me with a picture like that." With my spoon I stirred through the broccoli sauce. My thoughts went back to the moment I saw someone standing outside from our window, to what had happened outside. I shook my head. To be honest, I didn't know what was going on. The emotional part of me believed Ashley completely, because that meant I wasn't crazy, but the logical part of me said there were a lot of other explanations. Even if I couldn't name them right away. I noticed that Lea was no longer responding to that. "Do you believe it?"

She bit her lower lip.

"Lea, I won't laugh at you if you do believe it, you know that, right?"

She sighed and turned to me. "It's just...ever since we've been here there seems to be something heavy pressing into me. Like a thick blanket was thrown over me as soon as we walked in the house to keep me trapped here. As if it wants me to be aware of its presence. I try to shake off the feeling every time, but it doesn't work. I don't know how to explain it."

I put the spoon away and walked over to her. "Lea." I wrapped my arms around her waist and she placed her head against my chest. Her arms trembled slightly and she exhaled shakily. She felt cold. Concerned, I rubbed her back. She also had this stab in her chest earlier. I think she was really not doing well. I would do anything I could to take that feeling away from her. She deserved so much good, even if she didn't realize it herself. Always so selfless, she put others above herself too often and wanted to make sure that everything went well, that everyone had a good time. Unfortunately, she often neglected herself in the process. Just like now. She had planned the entire vacation, wanted everyone to enjoy it, but it didn't go as expected and then weird things happened. Lea was already a sensitive type, but this really hit home. I had never heard her talk like this about anything before.

After a while the trembling subsided and I pressed

a kiss on the crown of her head.

"Are you okay again? Do you think the sting from before has anything to do with this?"

She took a deep breath and shook her head. "No, I don't think so, but I'm fine again."

"Lea, you're picking up too many energies from others again." She had once told me that she was sensitive to the moods of others. She only had to walk into a room and immediately she could tell when someone was feeling unhappy, angry or sad. She also felt the opposite, but it was less present. Emotions that were perceived as negative overpowered the positive. Especially with the situation of Jill, Ashley and Dennis, I could well imagine it costing her energy. Then she would get cold, start shaking, and get tired.

"I know," she sighed. "But I can't help it."

"Didn't your mother teach you to shut yourself off? What did she say again?" In my memory I dug for her words. "Something about light, right?"

She nodded. "I had to put myself in a kind of spotlight. So that it seems like light surrounds me and forms an invisible barrier between me and the energies around me. Then all the feelings I experience are really mine."

"And grounding?"

Lea tilted her head and smiled. "I can't believe you remembered that."

That wasn't too hard. It sounded so complicated to me at the time that I just wanted to understand it. Grounding was done by standing with both feet on the ground. Her mother described it as letting roots shoot out of your feet to the center of the earth. In this way you were in touch with the facts and your head did not 'float' and overthink, as her mother described it. I understood the theory, not the execution. Still, it seemed to help Lea well and so I decided to memorize those things.

She snorted. "Oh, the meat!"

I turned around fast and turned off the fire. As soon as my nose hung over the pan, I smelled that it was just barely burned. That was a close call. "Is the food still salvageable?"

"Very safe." Lea picked up the pans and was already turning toward the dining room. "Then I think we can get to the table." I followed her with a few plates and coasters, then called out to the others that we could eat. A few fairly enthusiastic shouts sounded from the living room.

"It smells wonderful," Dennis said delightedly. "And this is why we let our responsible couple cook. Otherwise we'd be eating blackened food." He winked. That was also an exaggeration, but in some ways he was right. Lea did know how to do such things right.

One minute I was chuckling, the next the hairs on the back of my neck stood up. The temperature inside the house dropped and seemed to turn my blood to ice. The howling of the wind slowly turned into the sound of a crying baby. Everyone silenced.

As soon as a huge bang echoed through the house, the crying sound intensified. The bang caused even the lamps hanging above the dining table to vibrate. My gaze shot to Lea. I saw how the blood drained from her face, how a certain energy forced itself upon her. I reached out to her and grabbed her arm. Her blue eyes focused on me. With my eyes I tried to convey that everything was okay.

"That hatch again?" Dennis said. If he was at all affected by the slight change in the air, he didn't show it. "There I go again." He stuffed the potatoes still attached to his fork and walked toward the stairs. Before he put his foot on the first step, he turned to us. "Is anyone coming with me?"

"Can't you do it alone?" Jill asked with a slight mockery in her voice.

Dennis' knuckles turned white from the force with which he clamped the banister. I could see that Ashley wanted to say something, in fact her mouth opened, but she closed it again. Dennis sighed and walked upstairs. Even before the thought that it would have been nice if I had walked with him crossed my mind, he was gone.

Ashley puffed. "This house will give me a heart attack one day."

"Otherwise it will give me one," Jill said. "Just now, too, when you were all upstairs. Dennis suddenly jumped up, said he felt something and heard someone whisper his name." She poked at her food with her fork.

Above me, I heard Dennis' footsteps on the landing heading towards his room, just like last time. Something was probably wrong with the parts that were supposed to attach the shutter to the wall. I wanted to take another bite, but a loud bang behind me caused the meat to fall off my fork. Lea pushed her chair back in fright and turned her head in the direction of the sound. I, too, would like to know where it came from. The living room was suddenly a lot darker.

"Jesus Christ," Lea, who was sitting next to me, panted.

I looked at my friends, who were all looking around equally startled. Lea cringed as the hatch was blown open again.

"It's that hatch over there, I'll fix it." Jill's hands were shaking as she put her napkin on the table and walked to the living room. From there I heard, "Things are getting pretty intense outside. No wonder the shutters are jumping out of their locks." She fumbled at the window. Jill opened it and wet leaves immediately blew in. The map of the area that was on the table flew across the room.

I jumped up and rushed over to her. Half of Jill's body was already hanging out the window trying to reattach the shutter to the wall. With one hand I held her by her waist so she wouldn't fall, and with the other I made sure the window didn't slam shut and thus injure Jill. She had not yet closed the shutter and the window as another bang sounded.

"Oh, no way!" Jill yelled as she threw her arms in the air in frustration. "Now that other hatch. You know what? I'll fix them all right. What amateur fastened them in the first place this morning? Or attempted to?"

I made my way to the hatch that had just blown open. My eyes narrowed, I leaned out with my upper body to attach it to the outside wall. What clumsy things they were too. This house was old, but you would think that while renovating they could add modern materials. If this house had been renovated at all. Fortunately, I didn't live here.

"Wow!" I heard someone shout behind me.

'What is it?" I shouted back, as I could hardly understand Jill above the rushing wind.

"I just saved your life. The window was coming at you at full speed. The point would have seriously drilled right through you."

Exaggeration was also a skill. Groping around, I searched for the lock on the wall. *Found it*, I thought as I felt cold metal under my fingers. Soon I realized I had to look to know what I was doing.

Two intense black eyes were less than five inches from mine.

I stumbled backwards screaming. I tripped over my own feet, fell against Jill, and then landed on the ground with a loud crash. On all fours, I crawled backwards away from the window. It only took a few seconds, but in that short time I could see that she was young. That blood was flowing from her mouth and that she had hair that was blacker than the darkest night. Another scream left the back of my throat. And then she disappeared. She dissolved as if she had never been there.

I had seen that. I had really seen that. There was no more denying it was real. There was no more logical explanation. What Ashley had seen was real, what Dennis had felt was real and what I had seen in the garden and out our bedroom window...was real. She stood there and the next minute she disappeared into thin air. This girl was just not the woman we had seen standing in the garden, or the one I had seen out of my bedroom window. How many of them were watching us? And Ashley just now... Was anyone in the house already?

"Dennis," was the first thing that came to mind. Only now did I realize that Dennis should have been downstairs long ago, but I heard no sounds from upstairs.

"Kai, what is it?" Lea was standing next to me. I hadn't even noticed that everyone had gotten up. Jill was standing rubbing her rear end. She hadn't seen anything.

Panting, I ran to the stairs. "Dennis!" No answer. How long had we not heard from him? How long had he been gone? Now that I was upstairs by myself, I felt a lot less brave. The creaking of the wood was suddenly ominous, and the wind hitting the house sounded like shuffling footsteps. Every sigh I heard startled me, but everything turned out to be a false alarm. The image of the girl so close to my face was burned into my retinas.

With every step I took I feared the worst. I got closer and closer to his room, but not a sound indicated that anyone was there. "Dennis?" I asked again. "Is everything working out here?" I stood in the doorway.

All the lights were off. The window was closed, the shutter jammed. *At least he couldn't have fallen out*, I thought with relief. *But where was he then? Why didn't he answer?* I took a step further.

"Boo!" Dennis jumped out from behind the door and grabbed me by the shoulders from behind. My first reaction was a scream, then I pulled him off me and threw him onto the bed. He was a lot lighter than me, so I could easily handle his weight. Even after a volleyball game, I had never panted so hard. My heart was pounding in places I wasn't supposed to feel it.

"Dude, what's wrong with you!"

"Man, chill!" he roared, laughing. He clasped his stomach with his hands, a tear escaping the corner of his eye. Behind me, I heard a lot of rumbling and the girls stormed into the room.

"Kai! What the hell happened?" my girlfriend asked. Her red hair came into my field of vision.

"This idiot thought it would be funny to scare me." I gave him a shove after, which only made him laugh harder.

"You guys should have seen it; I kicked his ass so good! That look and then that scream. Hilarious."

I felt my cheeks glow. Lea put her hand on my forearm. Tingles shot through my body. I would do something to Dennis if it turned out he was behind everything. Lea took me out of the room, downstairs, where I reluctantly explained to her what I had seen outside the window. The situation wasn't exactly getting better.

Chapter 11

Jill

What was he going to do with that knife? My whole body stiffened in fear.

Lea's hands were shaking as she was busy washing the dishes. I took a plate from her and dried it off. Out of the corner of my eye, I took her in. She was paler than usual and her hair was tangled from constantly running her hands through it. Kai's story had scared her. And to be honest me too. He was always serious and when he said he had experienced something, we had to believe him.

The silence that hung between us in the kitchen could cut through the air. I desperately wanted to say something, but couldn't find the right words. And Lea looked as if a whole book of words would be rolling from her lips at any moment.

In the end, she was the one who broke the silence. "How are you?"

I had expected many things to come out of her mouth, but this question threw me off. "How do you mean?"

Lea handed me two forks. "Well, your situation with Ashley and Dennis doesn't seem too nice. I wanted to know how you are doing with that."

I shrugged. I didn't really know that myself. To be

honest, I tried to avoid thinking about it too much. "I'm okay," I eventually said.

"Okay."

Again, a silence fell between us.

It was clear to me that she was also trying to avoid a topic: the strange happenings in this house.

"And how are you?" Wow, this just seemed like the beginning of a WhatsApp conversation that was doomed to die.

"To be honest, I don't know." She heaved a deep sigh and looked at her reflection in a freshly washed plate. "I don't have them all in order anymore. It's such chaos, everything seems to be mixed up. I've lost track, like I can't think clearly," she confessed.

I raised my eyebrows. That was quite a confession. She normally discussed these things with Kai, but rarely with me. I didn't understand these things very well. Facts were facts and it didn't do you any good to keep fretting over things you couldn't do anything about. Was there a problem? Then you solved it. Was it beyond your control? Then there was no point in worrying about it. There was no problem? Well, fine.

"How annoying, Lea. Would you like to tell me what's going through your mind?" I could use that distraction. And it would probably relieve Lea.

"Well, you know. Even before this vacation started I was walking around feeling guilty because you guys had made out and I wasn't supposed to say anything about it. Then we arrived in a storm, then came your fight..."

Her rattling slowly faded into the background and

I sunk into my own thoughts. Lea not being able to think clearly anymore was a bad sign. She was the one who, on the contrary, always had them in order. I began to worry. Something about this environment was not good for her. I could see it in everything. Her attitude, her appearance, how much slower the words came out of her mouth.

My eyes wandered to the drawer to Lea's left, the one closest to the wall. Something in that area caught my attention. It took me a while to figure out what it was. The drawer was slowly being pulled out of the countertop. Centimeter by centimeter it slid outward. My eyes flashed to Lea's hands, but they were busy rinsing the dishes. She kept talking, not realizing that her words were no longer getting through to me.

I ceased my movement, looked back at the drawer and saw that the knives inside were reflecting the light from the ceiling lamp. Only then did I begin to see the outline of a hand. Hands that weren't supposed to be there.

My gaze went up along Lea's body, searching for the owner of that hand. Two large eyes that bulged too far from their eye sockets looked straight at me. The muscles in my body slackened and the plate I was holding slipped through my fingers. Just before the plate hit the ground and shattered into hundreds of pieces with a deafening sound, the light of a bolt of lightning flashed through the house. Startled, I looked down at the plate that had fallen, then at the thunder.

I breathed too fast and felt myself getting lightheaded. With my hands I clasped the edge of the countertop. My knuckles were turning white from the force I was putting on them.

"Jill?" A few seconds passed before I realized that Lea had already called my name several times. The black spots that had appeared before my eyes faded away and the world around me became clear again. Stunned, I looked up at Lea. This had never happened to me before. Had I almost fainted?

The appearance of a person behind Lea caused me to startle again, but in no time I calmed down. "Kai," I sighed. I suppressed the urge to put my hand on my heart. It was just Kai.

He pushed the drawer that held the knives closed.

"What are you doing here?" was the first question that came out of my mouth.

"I heard something break, so I came to see if everything is okay."

"Okay." That explained everything, he was here and... Wait a minute. I saw the hand and the face before I dropped the plate. It couldn't be. It wasn't possible. I didn't believe in such things, it didn't exist. I swallowed.

"Jill, what is it?" Kai asked.

"Nothing," I answered immediately. My standard answer when someone asked me if something was wrong. I didn't want them to know how badly I was shocked. I took a step back and heard the glazed ceramic of the plate creak under my shoes.

"There's something," Lea said.

"I was startled by the flash, sorry. I'll clean it up right away." I was already stooping to grab the brush and can from the kitchen cupboard, but Lea stopped me.

"No way. Do you think I'm stupid?" She put her hands to her sides and looked at me sternly. "Do you think I didn't realize you dropped the plate before the lightning bolt was even seen?" Lea raised her eyebrows as if she were my mother who had caught me while grabbing an extra cookie. That look made it impossible for anyone to lie.

I looked from Lea to Kai and back again. In my opinion, I had no choice. I sighed defeatedly and with drooping shoulders I said, "Didn't you see the drawer open?" I pointed at it.

"No."

"Someone pulled open the drawer, Lea. It wasn't you and me, Kai wasn't even in this room yet, and the eyes I saw were not Kai's. For a moment I thought it was him, but the man I saw had a light complexion."

Lea's arms fell limp along her body. "Right behind me? And I didn't notice anything." She put her hand in front of her mouth. "At any moment, someone could be standing behind you. You could just be attacked and you wouldn't even realize it until it was too late." Kai, meanwhile, spun around his axis, as if to make sure the coast was clear. "I want to get out of here," she called out. "Now, Kai, I don't like this anymore."

Kai immediately wrapped his arms around her. "I know, I know." He stroked her back reassuringly.

I watched the loving scene for a moment before I decided to clean up the shards. As I crouched down, I caught parts of their whispers.

"We'll confer with the others and leave as soon as

the storm passes. It's far too dangerous to drive along a cliff in this wet weather."

"But that will take until at least the middle of the night."

"I know, we'll leave tomorrow, I hope. I'll be with you tonight."

A sob left Lea's throat. "I'm just feeling so tired ever since I got here."

"I know."

If I had to hear 'I know' come out of Kai's mouth anymore, I'd beat him up. *Say something more useful than just 'I know,'* I thought. But for Lea, it seemed to work. I tossed the shards into the trash can. I recovered and looked straight at them.

"Let's go to the others in the living room. We need to confer."

They agreed and the three of us walked over to them. I took a seat next to Ashley on one couch and Lea and Kai sat down next to Dennis on the other couch.

Kai cleared his throat, causing Dennis and Ashley to look up from their phones. "We need to talk."

Ashley raised her eyebrows, and Dennis made an arm gesture that meant to say he could go ahead.

"We're leaving as soon as we can. As soon as the storm subsides, we're leaving this house."

No one asked why, no one questioned it. Instead, Ashley sank back into the couch in relief. Dennis nodded benevolently.

"I want to go home so badly," Ashley mused. "I hate it here."

Anger bubbled up inside of me. Such a hypocrite. "Ash, you're the one who brought us here!"

Immediately she sat up straight. "Hey, my parents recommended this place! How was I supposed to know all of this?"

I rolled my eyes. No, it was never Ashley's fault. Always pointing the finger at someone else. "And you or your parents didn't think it was worth checking the state of the house? Have you ever been here at all?"

She shook her head.

I raised my voice. "Have your parents ever been here?"

"Not that I know of," she squeaked.

Groaning, I put my face in my hands. The heat rose to my head. "Ever seen pictures of this place?"

'Yes!" she cried as if she had hit the jackpot. That only made my irritation grow. "They showed me a picture of the house. It was nice and big, that was all they knew too, so it made sense for us to go here so we could save money, right?" She twirled a lock of her blonde hair around her index finger. At first glance she seemed cute, sweet and even shy, but when you got to know her better you found out she was the opposite. Well, she was insecure, but that didn't manifest itself in the characteristics of sweet and shy.

"And what year was that picture from?" I asked on.

She shrugged again.

"Never mind, Jill. There's nothing that can be done about it now anyway," Kai came between us. His low voice somehow had a calming effect on me. "No point in pointing fingers."

I crossed my arms. There was no point, but it was nice to know that Ashley had gotten us into this mess.

"I have an idea!" After Dennis had given Kai quite a scare, he seemed his old self again. I pretended to hate it, but secretly I enjoyed it immensely. Especially when I could join in with his pranks. Unfortunately, my head was not into it at the moment. The man's eyes kept flashing through my head. Those eyes didn't even seem human. A shiver slid down my spine. No, don't think about it, please. Distraction, that's what I needed. Maybe it would help Lea, too.

"Tell me," I encouraged Dennis.

"Cards Against Humanity, but with booze. So whoever lays down the best card has to take a sip of his booze. It's late enough to drink alcohol."

That was true, we had eaten late tonight. I glanced at the clock. It had already been eight o'clock. That would been Lea and I had taken quite a long time to do the dishes.

Dennis with his great ideas. "I'm in!" I called out.

Ashley, Lea and Kai agreed as well.

I thought Cards Against Humanity was a fun game. One person drew a card with a sentence on it with blank spaces that had to be filled in. Then the other players put cards on the table that were meant for the blanks. The game contained the most ridiculous and provocative sentences and words, so that was promising.

Chapter 12

Ashley

He was skinnier than most of the men I knew, but since he didn't do much physical labor, that made sense.

After a few hours and a few beer bottles, everyone was pretty tipsy. This was how our vacation was supposed to be. We were doing very well. The storm was getting even fiercer than it already was – if that was at all possible – and the dark day had given way to a dark night. The wind that blew through the cracks of the house stroked along my arms. Compared to when we arrived, it had cooled off considerably. With a head full of cotton wool, I tried to concentrate on the game. Somehow, Cards Against Humanity was very addictive. There was something about putting offensive things together without anyone judging you. It was better than what I had experienced in the past few days. They often kept it to themselves, but I did notice how they looked at me. Like I was the only one who had done something wrong.

Lea put a card on the table.

"Oh, Lea, I didn't expect this from you," Jill laughed when it turned out that Lea had put down the winning card.

I raised my eyebrows at the sight of her card. Damn, that one was even in the stack of cards at all.

"I know quite well how to win this game," she said with double-talk. "And there's more to this than meets the eye." She pointed to her body and laughed. It was only when she had her drink that she became so loose. The girl who kept everything under control and sometimes took on the mother role in the group was gone.

I too began to notice that the drink was going to my head. Everything seemed just a little slower and I felt like I was floating above the couch.

"I do know what's behind it." Kai winked.

Lea's cheeks immediately turned red. She gestured for him to stop making those comments.

"Ugh." I moved my eyebrows up and down. "That is going to be a fun night, Lea, when Kai starts like that already." It was no secret that Lea and Kai had shared the bed more often – just this afternoon – but joking about it was still entertaining.

"Everything in the house is creaking," Jill said. She hiccupped. "So the bed probably does too. Then I'll have," hiccup, "no," hiccup, "good night's sleep." Hiccup.

"Yes, just like this afternoon." I thought about it, Dennis said. He winked after it.

Lea hid her face behind her hair and placed two hands on her cheeks as she giggled. Yeah, that one definitely had some alcohol in her system. The weird thing was that right now she seemed a lot fitter than she had just been. Healthier. The color was back in her face, somehow her eyes were bright and she was laughing carefree at the jokes of others.

Kai was smiling so wide that I could see his teeth. Even through his dark skin I could see that he was blushing. He pulled Lea closer to him and she pressed her forehead against his shoulder.

Booze makes people talk freely. The only one who didn't suffer from this was Dennis, because he took small sips carefully and made sure to drink enough water and eat snacks in between. He couldn't handle alcohol. It was a good thing he knew that himself and took it into account. I remembered a party from which he cycled home vomiting, only to suffer a hangover for two days, followed by a migraine attack that unfortunately for him lasted a few days.

"Okay, Ashley, your turn," Dennis said. *Partly to save Kai and Lea from the situation*, I thought. A breeze blew through the house and pulled me out of my daze. For a moment the drink had banished all problems from my memory, but now everything came crashing in like a thunderclap. What we had all been through, the fact that we were about to go upstairs to sleep. That I had to sleep alone. I felt a lot less like it now.

I took a sip of my beer. My throat felt as dry as sandpaper. And although I was getting cold, my skin felt way too warm. "I don't want to sleep alone tonight." The words were out of my mouth before I could stop them.

The other four looked up, suddenly a lot more serious than they had just been. Additional lines had formed on their foreheads as they frowned, and the cozy atmosphere that had been there before had instantly disappeared. Dennis wouldn't let me sleep in his room, he was still angry with me, despite the fact that he had started behaving more normal as the day had progressed. The same was true for Jill. And I didn't want to put Lea and Kai through that I would be sleeping in their room, which meant it wouldn't just be the two of them. But surely I couldn't be the only one who didn't dare?

"You just sleep in your own room. All of us," Jill said.

"What, you've seen for yourself what's in here!"

"Yes, I know, but nothing happened. We got startled a few times. Then again. None of us got hurt."

I found her comments very light-hearted for someone who had just come into the living room with a deathly pale face. I naturally touched the finger where I normally wore my ring. A stab went through my heart when I remembered that I had lost it, that we had not found it. Immediately the image of the woman we had seen standing in front of the house came back. I shook my head to banish that thought.

"All right, you know what?" Jill continued. "Everyone leaves their doors open tonight. Your room is right across from mine and the hallway isn't very wide, so we can keep an eye on each other and call out as soon as something happens. Is that an idea?"

Sleeping with the door open? I have hated that as long as I can remember. During my childhood, I had the idea that everyone could watch me while I slept. Right now, the idea of an open door gave me peace of mind and a sense of security.

"Okay," I agreed. If this was the best they could

come up with, I had to take it.

The rest agreed too, though it was with some doubt in their voices. Lea and Kai had the least to fear; the two of them were in the same bed and only needed to put out an arm to warn the other. I cast a stealthy glance at the couple. Jealousy bubbled up in my insides.

"I'm going to bed," Jill announced. She stretched excessively, to the point where I could hear a bone cracking in her neck or back. "You guys too?" She got up and went behind the couch, halfway to the stairs.

"Yeah." I followed her lead, but didn't dare go upstairs yet without the others. Hopefully they were ready to face a night of sleep as well. Or no, actually I was hoping that they all magically didn't dare at all and suggested that we all sleep in one room. Just like in the old days during sleepovers. All the mattresses on the floor against each other, more pillows and blankets than were necessary and fall asleep together. Unfortunately, no one suggested that and everyone headed off to their own domain with some hesitation. I didn't dare suggest it myself after Jill's reaction. They would make fun of me. I already felt so useless, terrible, and presumptuous.

On the way up, it seemed like there was lead in my shoes. My steps were labored and the speed of my heartbeat increased as I continued up the stairs. I still shared the bathroom with Dennis. Because of the mess in my room, the entrance to the bathroom was blocked from there, so I had to go through the hallway. Not a bad thing in itself, but it felt significantly colder there.

Dennis. Tomorrow I would talk to him again. I wanted this to work out. He was such a wonderful person and I could hardly live without him. It would break my heart if he decided it was over between us for good.

While brushing my teeth, I didn't dare look in the mirror. Since the moment I had seen the woman with the white eyes in it, I avoided that thing like the plague. Yet it beckoned to me, challenged me to take a look. I steadfastly refused. Quickly I spit the toothpaste into the sink and drank a sip of water. Dennis did the same. I waited until he was gone to pee. I purposely kept my face down to avoid accidentally looking in the mirror.

I had heard somewhere that fear made the powers of a dark spirit stronger. That they could then get more done in the physical world. A shiver rolled down my spine. *Don't think about that*, I thought. *I'm not afraid, I'm not afraid, I'm not afraid.* I breathed in and out deeply, flushed the toilet and walked down the hallway to my room.

The landing seemed like an infinite black hole. No lights were burning anywhere, which meant that everyone else was already in bed, trying to get some sleep. I glanced into Jill's room as I stood in front of mine. She was lying in her bed with her back to the door. I sighed deeply and walked into my room. I left the door open, as the others had thankfully done. Not much later I too had crawled under the covers, waiting for a sleepless night.

I didn't know how I had fallen asleep or what had wakened me. Something had caused my body to be in a state of readiness. Still with my eyes closed, I listened intently for sounds that didn't belong here. I heard the creaking of the ceiling, the rustling of the wind through the cracks, the thunder and...creaking on the landing.

In the silence of the night, the creaking of the wood caused by footsteps sounded like additional thunderclaps. Before I could form any coherent thought at all, my neck hairs stood up. Silently I pulled the blanket up to my chin and made myself as small as possible.

A little voice in my head spoke to me rationally. Someone probably had to go to the bathroom. Or they couldn't sleep and were getting a glass of water. But why did they go across the hallway if there was a direct connection to the bathroom from their room? Maybe they were checking each room to see if everyone was asleep. One thing I knew for sure was that what I heard was not to my liking.

The footsteps followed each other slowly and sometimes paused, as if the person was standing still from time to time. And if my sense of distance and time was any indication, I could swear they stopped at every open bedroom door.

I gave myself courage. I had to open my eyes to convince myself that it was one of my friends.

I immediately regretted that. As I looked at the doorway and waited for one of my friends to stop at my door, I saw something that seemed to come straight out of a nightmare.

The footsteps moved toward my door. The shoes that emerged were black lacquered. A pair of dark brown slacks enveloped the legs and the man who appeared before me was dressed in a neat shirt.

I looked up even further.

His cheeks were deeply sunken and his eyes seemed to bulge from their sockets. A stubble marred his face as it accentuated his protruding bones and a top hat concealed his hair. Worst of all? Although I saw him clearly, I could see right through him. I saw Jill's dark room through his body as if I were looking through clear water.

His eyes found mine. Looked straight at me. A smile broke through on his face. The corners of his mouth almost reached his eyes and the teeth were crooked.

He raised his arm. Only not in my direction, but in that of the door. As if stiffened, I watched. The door swung slowly in his direction. And very softly, so softly that even the vampires from series and movies would hardly be able to perceive it, the door fell into the lock.

My blood suddenly became ice cold, because I knew exactly who he looked like.

Chapter 13

Kai

"This world is no place for special people like us. People don't understand us, we could have it much better."

Lea's body warmed my skin. I felt her breathing and how she moved her head slightly to assume a more comfortable position. From the sound of her breathing, I could tell she was in a deep sleep. I also felt her hand rest lightly on my chest and her toes tickling my feet. I wanted to put my arm around her, hold her gently and fall asleep with her that way.

But I couldn't.

Literally.

My body lay numb in bed. My nerves worked so well that I could feel every breeze that brushed along my arm, but my muscles did not. They didn't give in by a millimeter. No matter how hard I tried to lift my hand, turn my head to the right or left, it was not possible. I couldn't even move a finger.

Panic was creeping in. Why couldn't I move?

I could only roll my eyes back and forth under my closed eyelids. I didn't want to open them, because I felt someone was watching me, studying me.

I took a rushed breath, my heart beating faster and faster. Drops of sweat rolled down my temples over my forehead.

Lea, I wanted to call out, but I couldn't speak. Not swallow. The only thing left that seemed to work were my heart, lungs, and eyes.

A strange sensation on my upper arm made me even more aware of my surroundings. Drip, drip, drip. What was that?

I opened my eyes and sucked in a sharp gulp of air when I saw it. When I saw her.

Lying on my back, staring at the ceiling, I tried to wake Lea up, to reach her. For up against the ceiling, right above me, she hung. She stared at me with wide-open eyes, her skin as white as snow, the skin around her eyes stained deep black. There seemed to be black veins running down her face, into her neck, down her arms and legs. Her white dress would have been dainty if it weren't torn to pieces and dangling above my paralyzed body. Her black hair hung down her face like long cloths, and her nails had carved into the ceiling behind her, as if she were holding herself up that way. It took me a moment to realize that this was a young girl. That this was the girl I had seen outside the window.

She opened her mouth. Blood seeped out and landed on my arm. Her jaw didn't seem to be attached to her face, so it stretched far and her mouth became a big, gaping black hole. Her eyes spread open even further.

A silent scream was on my lips as she let herself fall. Suddenly everything was moving very fast. Before she landed on top of me, she stretched her arms out to me.

I squeezed my eyes shut, but I felt nothing at the moment she would come down on me. I did, however, feel a sharp sting in my upper arm.

High pitched giggles moved around the room and I opened my eyes just in time to see her standing in the doorway looking at me. With a wide smile and tilted head, she studied me intensely. She raised her hand slowly, as if to wave.

And then the door fell shut.

Chapter 14

Dennis

At first, I couldn't believe it, thought I could resist it, my impending death.

I turned onto my side, facing the door. Apparently, someone had decided to take a night trip. Slowly I opened my eyes, rubbing out the sleep. Did they have to be so loud? I regretted leaving the door open. I had to look twice and frowned when I saw that Kai and Lea's bedroom door was closed. I chuckled. Maybe they had decided they wanted some privacy for their nightly activities after all. Fine with me, I was already relieved that I hadn't witnessed any of it.

Sighing, I turned onto my other side. But as soon as I did, I noticed the pressing sensation of my bladder. I groaned. That always happened when I woke up in the middle of the night.

I slapped the covers off me and immediately the freshness of my room made me shiver for a moment. The storm was still raging outside and it didn't seem like it had any intention of moving away anytime soon. I stood up and took a step.

I fell before I realized what was going on. My head was spinning from the impact and I screamed. Loudly.

The pressure around my ankle was unmistakably that of an icy hand. I looked back. A livid white hand encircled my ankle from under my bed and pulled me towards it with a brutal force.

I scratched the floor with my short nails. As I struggled violently, my lower legs disappeared under the bed.

"Help!" I cried out at the top of my lungs. As I kicked with my foot, I hit something. The only reaction I got was giggles.

One hand gave way to two hands around my calves. They crept further and further up my legs, to the hollows of my knees, my thighs. An icy sensation went through my body.

I had no control over my body anymore, it felt like I was being jerked in all directions. I couldn't see anything except the hands and forearms.

The nails were pressing into my skin, leaving prints.

"Help!" I cried even louder. My voice skipped.

"Dennis," I heard from the doorway.

My head shot up. I thought one of my friends who had heard my shouts was standing there, but in the doorway stood a man. He looked like he had just stepped out of a time machine. His clothes were old and his face was so thin that he looked malnourished.

As soon as the man uttered my name, the grip around my ankles tightened. The bottom of the bed scraped across my lower back. Only then did I realize that already half of my body was pulled under the bed. No, man, no! I was terrified as I looked up at the man.

His eyes bore into mine. I couldn't find the strength to look away. As I struggled to get myself out of the grip of the hands, I prayed that this would be over soon and that I would wake up in my bed, laughing at myself for this nightmare. But the fierce stings of the nails pressing harder and harder into my skin told me that I was not dreaming.

I was wide awake.

A grin appeared around the man's lips and he walked towards me with slow steps. At this point I didn't know if I wanted to crawl forward to get away from the hands, or backward to get away from the man. But it was already too late. He was standing right in front of me, looking down at me.

Warm tears streamed down my cheeks. "Don't hurt me," I begged. It was useless, I realized as soon as I felt the side of the bed cause scrapes on my back. Only my shoulders and head were still sticking out from under the bed. This was not how my life was going to end.

The man sank through his knees until his face was right in front of mine. Although I could see his insane eyes, I looked straight through them.

He came closer and closer.

The door slammed shut with a bang.

One last, firm tug and I was pulled completely under the bed.

Chapter 15

Lea

"For you I have something special in store."

I wasn't myself. I knew that from the moment I took a step into the dark room. Everything seemed so surreal, a dream. Usually I was the main character in my dream, but I noticed from everything that this was not my own body. Normally I looked at all events from a higher perspective, this body was smaller. I had no control over it.

At first, I couldn't see a hand in front of my face. Foot by foot I shuffled forward. The paralyzing feeling of fear spread through my body. My legs softened and I began to sweat profusely.

A hand on my back urged me to continue walking. The push caused me to fall forward and almost trip over an object that was in the way. The hand grabbed the top of my dress and held me upright, pulling me against him. A male hand rubbed up my back, to my neck, where his fingers touched my skin. The compelling feel of his fingers made its way to my throat. With his sharp nail, he scratched a shallow gash in my skin, gently and cautiously. The silent warning could not be clear enough. Somehow I knew he was my husband, the wedding ring on his finger confirmed it.

I swallowed. I had to suppress the urge to jump

away and run, far away from him. But I didn't have to look back to know that I was stuck, that I had nowhere to go.

I thought back to what had happened up there, outside the door that led to the basement, and intense sadness flooded me. A kind of sadness I had never known before. I had been powerless.

I shook my head wildly. Something wasn't right. What sadness? What had taken place? Before I could get my thoughts in order, other thoughts seemed to take over mine again.

Suddenly the room was lit by the dim light of a candle he had just lit and held in his hand, allowing me to see the dust particles swirling through the air.

He had not let go of my dress. With a compelling motion, he led me through the dusty basement. Not in a million years had I thought he would be capable of something so gruesome that even the dead turned over in their graves.

At the very back of the basement he stopped. He placed the candle on a chest that had been there for as long as I could remember and moved the cabinet.

My body felt like it was frozen. I touched my skin. It felt cold. I couldn't feel my lips as I tried to form the words, so I said nothing. I took a small step backwards, with difficulty. As I nearly sank through my knees, I only noticed how uncontrollably I was shaking.

"Stand still!" he hummed.

Without thinking I did what he said. Like I always did. And it was precisely in this state that I knew I better listened to my husband.

With heavy panting and a whole lot of groaning, he managed to move the cabinet inch by inch. When the cabinet was out of the way, he picked up the candle. The light showed me a square piece of wall that looked different from the rest.

He looked at me, a big grin appearing on his face. Normally I loved that smile, but now it scared me in a way it hadn't before. With a hefty thrust of his arm against the wall, the brick crumbled. He grabbed my arm roughly and pushed me out in front of him into a dark room. A hallway. I had no idea this room was under our house.

I didn't want to realize it, but deep down I knew I was walking towards my death.

With a jolt, I shot upright. I groped my body, which was once again my own. Sighing, I let myself fall back into the mattress. Normally I didn't dream as if it were real. To reassure myself, I nestled against Kai, who lay dead still beside me. As I laid my head on his chest, I noticed how his heart was racing. Just like his breathing.

Frowning, I looked up. "Kai?"

The only window in the room was occasionally lit by a lightning bolt, so I saw that his eyes were open. He looked at me, but didn't move. The fear in his eyes gave me the chills.

"Kai, what is it?"

His eyes flashed to the door.

I looked up. "Closed. But how?" Suddenly a shiver rose from my lower back, up my spine, to my neck. An uneasy feeling crept up on me. The door was closed and something was wrong with Kai.

"Say something!" Panicked, I shook him. My eyes fell on his other arm, where there was a red color. Blood. "Kai!"

His whole body was shaking, until his head suddenly came up. I was startled by his sudden movement. He moved his arms and upper body. From his throat came a sound that could best be described as a mixture of a sob and a groan.

I waited, perhaps he needed time. I had never seen him so anxious. His face looked livid, as if he had seen a ghost.

I got down on my knees beside him and rubbed his clammy back reassuringly.

"I was paralyzed, I couldn't move, I was seeing things," he said, stammering.

"Sleep paralysis?" He had never told me he suffered from that.

He wiped the sweat from his neck. "I think so, but what I saw seemed so real. It is real." His eyes got big. "It's exactly the same girl I saw outside the window!" He nodded in the direction of the door.

An ominous feeling settled in my lower abdomen. I got up from the bed and tiptoed to the door. I gave it a tug and pushed, but it was stuck. After another attempt, I came to a chilling conclusion.

"We're locked in."

Chapter 16

Jill

I couldn't stand it any longer.

The sandman didn't seem to want to step by tonight. I had been tossing and turning in my bed for hours, unable to sleep. The storm was still raging as vigorously as it had during the day and with each thunderclap I was drawn back to the here and now instead of to dreamland, where I so desperately wanted to be. After shifting position for the umpteenth time, I sat up straight in bed out of pure frustration. I pricked up my ears. Someone was walking loudly down the hallway, not bothering to be quiet. I had to look twice and frowned when I saw that Ashley's bedroom door was closed. What was her problem? First she whined about not wanting to sleep alone and agreed with the suggestion to leave the bedroom doors open, and then she closed hers. What a hypocrite. Inwardly I scolded her. I would say something about this tomorrow. I didn't care that there might be an argument.

I ran my hands through my hair. Maybe drinking a glass of water would help with the restlessness and my frustration.

The wood felt cold under my bare feet. Calluses scuffed across the floor as I slowly made my way to the bathroom.

I filled a glass with water and immediately took a sip. At least the coolness did me some good. A huge bang announced that my bedroom door had been slammed shut, causing me to immediately spit out the water. I coughed and turned around. There was no one standing in my room. Who decided to close my door in the dead of night?

I turned and reached for my towel to wipe my mouth. The phantom in the corner of my eye startled me. Without any warning, my body stiffened. I saw movement in the mirror that hung in front of me. I didn't want to look, but I needed to know who was in the bathroom. Maybe I should just go back to my bedroom and leave the mirror for what it was. But I couldn't. Not even after everything that had happened today.

And so I raised my head.

I looked into two bright eyes. The dead white face was staring at me from the mirror. The woman across from me, with the long black hair, just stood there and looked straight at me. Shivers spread throughout my body.

I regained control of my body and flinched. I bumped against the edge of the closet.

She raised her hand and brought it toward the mirror. As if trapped on the other side of the glass, the tip of her finger pressed against the mirror. Her finger moved, trying to write something.

I didn't wait to see what the outcome was. No way I was going to read how she was going to kill me. I sprinted out of the bathroom and slammed the door behind me. Like a man possessed, I yanked on the latch of my bedroom door, but it wouldn't budge. I was stuck. My heart was pounding in my throat as I glanced back at the bathroom door. I expected to see her there in the doorway at any moment.

The sound of a laughing baby came from the bathroom.

"Guys!" I called out.

Chapter 17

Ashley

I had been powerless no matter how hard I tried.

Barely two minutes after my door had slammed and I had stayed in bed curled up like a ball, I heard noise everywhere. Doors slamming, Dennis screaming for help, Jill calling out to us, and I thought I heard Kai and Lea stumbling through their room. I had made the choice quickly. I threw the covers off me and made a dash for the door. The handle was ice cold and didn't budge. The doors to the hallway had no lock, so why didn't it open? Oh my goodness.

My heart hammered against my ribcage. "Jill!" I called out when I heard her scream.

"Ashley?" she called back.

"What's going on?" I asked.

"I have no idea, but we need to-" She stopped talking for a moment. I think I heard Kai yell something. I listened carefully to see if I heard Lea and Kai shouting. They were, but it was too soft and too far away to make out any decent words. I could only assume what Jill was shouting back, and in doing so, imagine what they were saying. "Yes, do it!" she shouted a moment later.

"What's he going to do?" I continued to tug at the latch. "My door won't open!"

"Mine won't either, Kai is going to kick in the doors," Jill said.

"Dennis?" I called out. No answer. "Dennis!" I tried again, but still nothing. I walked over to the wall that bordered our shared bathroom and pressed my ear against it. "Dennis, can you kick in the door as well?" No answer, I didn't hear him. My heart sank to my feet and I ran back to the door only to pull on it even harder than before. Just a moment ago he had screamed. He had to be able to hear us.

"Guys, something's wrong with Dennis, he's not answering!" I shouted in a state of panic.

Somewhere I expected Jill to remark that Dennis was probably playing a joke, but instead she said, "Okay, but first the door. We can't help him until we get out ourselves." There was a tremor in her voice that wasn't normally there. Not with Jill. Jill was never afraid.

A thump echoed through the house, but not the sound of breaking wood. That was probably Kai trying to kick the door open. Attempt one had failed. Two more punches followed, until the fourth was accompanied by creaking, the sound of breaking wood and a groan from Kai.

"Are you out?" Jill shouted.

"Yes!" Kai's voice was suddenly a lot clearer. Pain echoed in his voice. Being in this situation was bad enough, but if he had been hurt, we were even further from home.

Home. How badly I wanted to be there right now. Comfy in my own bed, a blanket over my head and pretending this had never happened. As if I still had a happy relationship with Dennis, as if I had never kissed Jill, and as if we weren't being hunted in our vacation home. My family home.

With difficulty, I remained standing at the door. I was terrified that the man would return, perhaps wanted to keep me away from the door. The doors were sealed for a reason: he had deliberately locked us in. The thought that I was standing in the exact same spot where he had been less than a few minutes ago terrified me.

From the way they were walking, I could hear Kai and Lea coming my way and stopping at my door. "Is there a crowbar or something else long and hard in your junk room that won't break if you try to break the door open with it?"

"Um," my eyes scanned the room. "I'll go look." I looked for the light switch in the room and soon found it. Why hadn't I turned on the light right away? Sometimes I made myself go insane. With a rocking speed I rummaged through boxes, closets and dark corners. When my hand touched something hard and cold, I knew I had got something. "Gotcha!"

"Nice, what is it?" he asked.

"Just a steel beam. There's a box full of them here."

"Is there something in there with a protruding point? In the shape of a crowbar?"

I searched the box thoroughly. No object escaped my inspection. "No."

"Okay."

I could almost hear him thinking and suppressed the rising panic. "What do I do?" In my head I was already ramming the door at random. I had to get to Dennis as quickly as possible. He still hadn't said anything. What if something bad had happened?

The lights began to flicker. I stopped what I was doing and waited for it to stop, but it persisted. That didn't seem like the work of the storm to me. We had to hurry up. We had all seen enough horror movies to know this was wrong. "Hurry up!"

"Can you squeeze it between the door and the doorframe?" he asked.

I looked at the five-inch bar in my hands and at the gap that was barely an inch wide. My knuckles turned white as I balled my hands into fists around the beam out of sheer frustration. "No."

"Damn," he growled.

Yeah, you could say that, I thought. "Now what?"

"Stand as far away from the door as you can, I'll ram it in. Lea, just stand a little further away."

"Okay, watch out," Lea squeaked.

My feet carried me as fast as they could to the far corner of the room. As soon as I hit the wall, I felt cobwebs against my bare arms. I cringed internally. The air before my eyes became increasingly blurry and seemed to distort. A few seconds later, I was staring into a face that couldn't have been more than ten inches from mine. The black eyes studied me and a grin bulged his sunken cheeks slightly. Through him I saw the door. Slowly he came closer and closer. It felt like my throat was being squeezed shut. I couldn't get any air.

"Stay," I heard him say.

"No!" I scratched. With eyes closed, I grabbed at the air in front of me. I intended to push him away, to run around him, but I felt no matter. Only the bleak emptiness of air was in front of me. I did not open my eyes again. Not even when two ice-cold fingers stroked my tear-stained cheeks. I trembled on my legs.

"Ashley, I'm coming!" Kai shouted.

There followed a loud bang, and then the splintering of wood. I ducked and held my hands in front of my face. When I opened my eyes again, the man was gone.

Kai stepped towards me. "Come," was all he said. He reached out his hand to me. Trembling, I grabbed it. He dragged me out of the room with him.

"Jill?" he asked.

"Yes?

He placed his hands around the latch and pulled it down. The door did not yield the moment he pushed against it. Sweat beaded on his forehead.

"Finally," I heard her whisper on the other side.

I went to stand next to Lea and held her hand. We made sure we were far enough away from him. Lea squeezed my hand. Her whole body was shaking as much as mine. She looked livid, just like I probably looked.

I couldn't stay still because of the nerves and shifted my weight from one leg to the other. We had to get to Dennis as soon as possible. I would never forgive myself if we got to him too late and something had happened to him. Panic bubbled up inside me. I knew I needed to keep my cool, that I could think better that way, but I couldn't. I was never one to stay calm. How could I keep my cool when my boyfriend wasn't responding? Or...my ex-boyfriend.

Kai walked back a bit and estimated the distance between his leg and the door. He kicked right under the latch. The thing sticking out of the door into the frame jumped out and the door flew open. So an old house had its advantages after all; everything could be broken easily.

Jill stood against the wall on the other side of the room. "Seriously, finally." She ran out into the hallway and patted Kai on the shoulder briefly as a thank you before continuing to walk.

"Dennis," I whispered. "We have to get to Dennis!"

"That's where I am headed!" Jill cried. "Hasn't he kicked his door in himself yet?"

"No, he hasn't said a word the whole time!" I made a dash for his bedroom door, the room in which we had planned to spend a few romantic nights. I pounded on it with my fist. "Dennis!" I shouted. It remained silent on his end. I ran my hands through my hair. I broke out in a sweat. "Do something!" I shouted at whoever was there.

Jill pushed me aside and gestured to Kai and Lea - who were also there by now - to stay put. She kicked the door in without hesitation.

"If I had known I could do this I would have kicked my own door right in," she growled.

In front of us a dark room revealed itself. Jill was the first to run in, scanning the wall with her hands until she found the light switch. The light flicked on.

I scanned the room. The bedroom was empty, his bed was empty. The blankets were crumpled, as if he had just laid in them.

Jill ran to the bathroom. Kai walked into the room. As did I, and Lea remained hesitantly in the doorway. She looked worse by the second, as if she might faint at any moment.

"Kai, stay with Lea," I instructed him. She needed someone who literally stood by her side. "I'll find Dennis." This was nothing like me. I never took charge, I was never one to think rationally in panic situations. But somehow I was doing that now.

On the other side of the room was a huge closet. It would really be something for him to hide in there and scare us. Oh my god, how furious I would get if this was a joke. I would really hit him. On the other hand, I couldn't imagine him doing that after hearing us panic. I walked around the bed toward the closet. I pulled open the heavy doors. Nothing. The closet was empty. Where could he be?

Jill came running out of the bathroom. "He's not in there."

Once again I scanned the room thoroughly. I looked at the bed, studied every inch. I saw something lying on the floor, something just sticking out from under the bed. Shocked, I breathed in. It was fingers. I recognized his slightly chubby fingers by the calluses. With trembling legs I crept up to it. I couldn't bring myself to walk any faster.

My heartbeat quickened as I sat on my knees at the side of the bed. I gathered my courage and slowly bent down so I could see under the bed. My breath caught in my throat.

I looked straight into his eyes, but his eyes seemed to be looking right through me. In a reflex, I grabbed his hand. As soon as I felt his skin I knew he was no longer alive. It was colder, lifeless. No, this couldn't be. His soulless eyes didn't move.

"Dennis," I whispered. He didn't respond. "Dennis!" I shook him. He had to respond. "Wake up." Warm tears streamed down my cheeks. I didn't want to face the truth. It was impossible.

Someone came and sat next to me, shoved me aside a little and bent down to see for himself what I was seeing. I saw Kai's dark skin through my tears.

"I can't feel a heartbeat. He's not breathing anymore. Come on, man. Come on!" he cried.

Everything happened in a blur, as if in slow motion. I managed to pull myself to my feet and stand up. The world was spinning around me. His words thumped through my head.

I don't feel a heartbeat.

He's not breathing anymore.

Lea wanted to go to Kai, but he quickly got up and dragged her back to the door. "No, you don't want to see this." He turned to Jill. "Take her, wait outside."

"But...what's going on?" Lea asked in a trembling voice. "What happened?"

Kai said nothing, he just shook his head defeatedly.

"Wait in the hallway." He said it loudly, but the pounding in my head made it sound like a whisper. As soon as they were gone in the hallway, he ran back. He grabbed Dennis' wrist and pulled him out from under the bed.

With eyes wide open, I looked at Dennis' lifeless body. Like a rag doll, he was dragged across the floor. Deep purple-red marks around his throat contrasted sharply with his white skin.

I turned my face away. "What are you doing?" I sobbed.

"I need to resuscitate him, Ash! I'm not going to lose my best friend, do you hear me?"

A loud sob escaped me. "Kai, you can't, it's been a while since he..."

"Ashley! We have to resuscitate him. Help me."

Defeated, I lowered myself next to Dennis' body. I could tell from everything that he had been dead too long to be resuscitated. I looked up and my gaze crossed Kai's. Behind the tears, I saw hope shining. I didn't want to be the one to crush his hope. I couldn't believe it myself. It felt like my heart had been ripped out of my ribcage. It hurt so much. I looked again at Dennis' open eyes, which stared soullessly at the ceiling.

Kai had placed his hands on Dennis' chest as he relaxed just before he was about to begin CPR. His arms fell limply along his body and he himself fell backwards. With his hands he rubbed through his frizzy hair.

"No, no, no," he whispered. Tears glistened on his cheeks. "It's no use anymore."

That made me unable to contain my own outburst. The one for whom I had cared so much, who loved me despite all my flaws, was no longer here. No, this couldn't be true. I was torn between believing and not believing. As much as I wanted to, I couldn't take my eyes off his body. After all the police series I had seen, I knew he had been strangled. But this time there was no culprit you could arrest and throw behind bars. This had been done by something completely different. Something we couldn't explain. I moved my hand to my throat and thought back to the feeling of being deprived of air, of my throat being squeezed shut as the man stood right in front of me. Had I felt how my boyfriend had died? How the life was squeezed out of him?

A roar of laughter, a girlish giggle and a crying baby. All the sounds came in at the same time. It made my blood go ice cold.

My stomach turned over. I got up and sprinted to the bathroom. There all my stomach contents came up. Weakly I hung over the toilet bowl.

Dennis was dead.

Chapter 18

Jill

The silent warning couldn't be clear enough.

Ashley ran out of the bedroom. All the color had drained from her face and her cheeks were wet with tears. "We have to get out of here, now!" she cried as she stomped her foot on the floor.

From across the room, I heard Kai sobbing loudly. My heart was beating faster and faster. This could not be good news.

Lea, who had been standing very still next to me the whole time, started moving as soon as she heard Kai and walked into the room.

"No, Lea, don't..." began Ashley, but it was too late, judging by the scream Lea produced.

I turned my questioning gaze to Ashley. "Ash, what happened?" A lump formed in my throat when she told me about Dennis.

"He's dead, strangled!" She slapped her hands in front of her face and started breathing faster and faster. "He was under the bed and I saw him there and his eyes and he was dead and he had bruises and..."

I rushed to her and grabbed her hands, pulling them away from her face. "Ash, Dennis can't be dead. He can't be."

"And yet he is!" she shrieked. She sank to her

knees and landed on the floor crying.

I placed my hand on her shoulder and looked through the doorway into the room. From here I could only see his feet lying next to the bed. Lea was trying her best to get Kai up.

"How could this have happened?" I shouted.

Ashley was crying so hard she could barely speak. "He was strangled, he…"

Despite the fact that I would have preferred to cry on the floor like Ashley, my tears somehow didn't seem to want to announce themselves. My face was still dry. Only from the inside I was crying as hard as I could. It felt like my insides were being torn apart with grief. It just wasn't coming out. I wanted to go into the room, see for myself and verify that Dennis was really dead. What if Kai had jumped to a conclusion too quickly? That he couldn't think straight anymore and just assumed he was dead. I shook my head, as if I could banish that thought from my mind this way. There was only one thing to do: get out of here. I didn't care that it was dark outside, that it was still raining and storming like crazy. We were no longer safe here. Something was inside the house and it wanted us dead.

"Ash, get up," I said sternly.

She was startled by my tone so much that she did as I said. With the sleeve of her pajamas she wiped the snot from under her nose.

I hurried into the room with great strides. Words would not get Kai out of here. I focused only on Kai and Lea. I tried to keep Dennis' body out of my line of sight. When I did catch glimpses of it, I put the images far away in my brain. I stood behind Kai and crossed my arms under his armpits. With some difficulty - because he himself seemed to have no strength left in his legs - I pulled him up. Lea kept talking to him, kept insisting that we had to leave now.

"But Dennis… We can't leave him."

With a heavy heart I said, "Dennis is no longer there, Kai. We'll call people as soon as we get a signal, but we have to leave now, or they'll get us too." Come to think of it…it had been pretty quiet in the house this whole time. I saw no more apparitions and heard no sounds. *Please, let it stay that way*, I thought.

When Kai could stand on his own two feet, I gave him a shove and he walked out of the room. Lea and I rushed after him. I grabbed Ashley by her wrist and dragged her towards the stairs, with Kai and Lea following behind us.

"Wait!" Ashley cried. She ran to her room.

"Ash, we really don't have time to take stuff now. Come on!"

Less than ten seconds later she was back outside, holding up her phone. "We do need to be able to call people later."

"Okay, let's go."

Somehow Ashley seemed to have picked herself up and she ran down the stairs after Lea and Kai. I'd never experienced her when she was in an emergency situation, but I didn't expect her to be in such a state of mind.

Kai looked for the light switch, but when he found it, the lights didn't turn on.

"Did the storm knock out the power?" Lea asked. She shrugged.

The temperature in the room dropped. I wasn't the only one who felt it; the others looked up too. A shiver that ran down my spine made the hairs on my body stand up. I felt like I was being watched from every angle. Eyes burned on me. My breath caught in my throat as I felt fingers on my neck. It was none of my friends, because I was standing at the very back. There was no one standing behind me. There couldn't be. I refused to turn around. I refused to give in to that urge and maybe end up like Dennis. At that thought, I startled. No, I would not end up like Dennis. For him, I had to fight. I couldn't just let this happen to me! Before I could even think about it, I jabbed my elbow backwards, but I hit nothing but air and the fingers didn't disappear.

Lea looked wide-eyed at something just behind me.

I gathered up all my courage and said, "There's someone behind me, isn't there?"

She nodded slowly, then cringed as if in pain. "Someone is touching me," she whispered.

Right next to her was a girl. The presence behind me felt much larger than that and definitely not pleasant. Now that I was experiencing this, I realized that I hadn't felt so threatened in the bathroom. I thought about last night when, while washing dishes, I saw the drawer with the knives in it open. And the man standing next to Lea. The threatening feeling that seemed to radiate from it. That's what it felt like now. Every cell in my body was telling me that I was right, that this same man was standing behind me.

Ashley let out a scream and flinched. Kai, too, made movements as if to knock something off him.

Suddenly the fingers weren't just on my neck, they travelled all over my body, only to return to my neck. I struggled against it and kicked, but it had no effect. The fingers wriggled around my throat from behind. They pressed on my larynx. On my windpipe. Squealing, I sucked in air. With my hands I grabbed the fingers that were clasped around my throat. This time I could touch it. His hand around my neck was ice cold. I wasn't getting enough air. My throat was burning. My lungs were crying out for more oxygen. I did everything I could to heed it, but my airway was closed off. Black spots appeared before my eyes.

Kai stepped towards me and slammed something behind me. He was cursing. I didn't really realize what was happening around me, couldn't think clearly anymore. Slowly I sank into unconsciousness and I knew I would meet my end the same way Dennis did.

"Jill!" Ashley yelled. Suddenly I felt two arms around my body throwing me to the ground. Not much later, I heard a crash, followed by the sound of breaking glass.

Suddenly, I was getting enough air. I took a deep breath and grabbed at my throat. The fingers were gone. Air was able to flow back into my lungs, though it didn't feel like I could breathe normally again. Rasping, I asked, "What happened?"

"I have no idea, but suddenly an iron object flew through the man, against the glass in the kitchen."

"What?" I couldn't wrap my head around it. What was going on? Vaguely I heard noises around me. Things being moved, flying through the air. It was none of us. We were all here.

And then it stopped.

It was dead silent.

"I'm not staying here a second longer! Come with me." Kai flung open the door downstairs and wind and rain met me. Barefoot I stepped outside, into the mud. No one had put on any other clothes or shoes. We just wanted to get away as soon as possible. Away from this house and the people who wanted us dead.

We ran to the car that was parked next to the house under a roof and got in. Kai immediately turned on the engine and pressed on the gas pedal. Mud splattered up behind us and rain splattered on the windshield. At high speed we drove towards the gate. Kai pressed the keys to the gate into Lea's hands - don't ask me how, but somehow he had the keys to both the car and the gate with him - and said to me, "Help her."

Together with Lea, I stepped out into the stormy night. The wind that whizzed in my ears rose above all other noise. Although it was the middle of summer, my bare arms and legs were getting very cold.

I watched as Lea inserted the key into the lock, lowered the latch and pushed. Nothing. Not an inch of the gate moved.

"Did you open it properly?"

"Yes. It's no longer locked."

I pushed her aside a little too hard and tried to turn the keys, but the gate was indeed no longer locked.

"Then it's definitely clamping again, just like yesterday. Help me push!"

We put our feet firmly in the ground, as far as we could with the mud, and pushed with all the strength we had. Nothing.

Defeated, I turned to the car, which still had Kai and Ashley in it. I raised my shoulders and arms, to let them know something was wrong, but we didn't know what.

They got out of the car and helped push against the gate. A few moments later, when nothing had changed in the situation, Kai's face turned angry. He hit the iron with two flat hands and yelled out. "Damn it! This fucking thing! Let us go!"

"You guys can't leave until I want you to," Lea said.

I put on big eyes. 'What, Lea, what are you talking about?" Surely it couldn't be that she was behind this? Had she locked us in? It didn't take long for me to realize something was wrong.

Her voice sounded lower than normal and scratchy. Her eyes looked blurry and it seemed like she couldn't see us. She stood stiffly at the gate staring in our direction and remained silent for a moment.

"You stay here until I let you go, I want..." she said. Suddenly she seemed to regain control of her own body and as the tension drained from her body, she quickly wrapped her arms around herself. She shivered.

It took a few seconds for Kai to stand beside her. He cupped her face with his hands and whispered words to her that I couldn't hear from here.

Shocked, I stared at her. "Lea..." I began.

She shook her head in response. "We can't leave," she sobbed. "I felt it from the very beginning. That was what I felt, Kai. And she spoke to me, in my head. She keeps the gate locked. We can't go."

"What?" squeaked Ashley.

"Shit!" I put my hands to the back of my head and spun aimlessly on my axis. "If we can't leave, we have to go back inside."

"What?" repeated Ashley. "No, we can't go back, because then..."

"We can't stand here in the cold and rain either," Kai sighed. He held Lea tightly and led her to the car. "Get in, we have to go back."

A minute later we were back inside a warm, but dark house. I absolutely no longer felt safe within these four walls.

I slowly looked at the others. All were standing, on edge. My eyes scanned the room to assure myself that nothing really happened anymore. Almost naturally, we made our way carefully to the living room.

Apparently we all had the same idea, because we sat down on the couch at the same time. I was totally exhausted, it felt like my legs were made of pudding. Actually, the couch was just a little too small for four people, but we made sure it fit. Lea sat half on Kai and I was wedged between them and the banister.

I was still shivering all over my body. I even noticed that I was actually cold.

Lost in thought, I stared ahead of me. What was our next step? Surely we couldn't stay here? The events of last night haunted my mind and I blurted out, "I saw a woman in our mirror last night."

They looked up in response. Ashley gasped. "Could it be the same woman I saw?"

I shrugged. "It could be. The woman I saw had long, black hair and..."

"So did mine when I saw her in the mirror! Oh my god, it is the same woman."

Kai sighed deeply. "There was a girl hanging from my ceiling last night. She was young, blood was coming out of her mouth and when she fell, she scratched me." He showed his upper arm. The wound wasn't too bad, but the fact that he had also been physically attacked frightened me.

"I had nightmares about a basement, I think the one in this house, and a secret passageway behind it. But I wasn't myself, it was like I was in someone else's body and all my movements and thoughts had been taken over. I think I was the woman who was speaking from me out there."

"With me there was a man standing in the doorway, I heard him walking down the corridor beforehand. I think he stopped in front of all the bedroom doors to look at us. He closed my door. I was too scared to move or make a sound," she admitted.

I wanted so badly to have a logical explanation, but what good was that if you had seen the impossible for yourself? It couldn't be, yet it was true. Maybe there were people hiding in the house, in the walls for example, and they were scaring us for their own pleasure. Or we were in a movie like *The Cabin in the*

Woods. But Dennis was dead; a joke could never go that far. Right? And could all those other things be explained?

God, at this point I hoped we were simply being pranked. Because if we weren't, I didn't know if I could handle that.

Real ghosts. That was Lea's explanation. Unfortunately, I could relate to that. But ghosts...they only existed in books and movies. It was impossible. And yet I had seen it myself.

"Aren't ghosts only supposed to appear around twelve o'clock at night?" I asked. "That's the case in all those stories, isn't it?"

"No. I've read that around three o'clock at night it's so dark that they are strong enough just then," Lea said.

"But then how do you explain that all those strange things were already happening during the day?"

Lea shrugged and looked at me. "It was very dark because of the storm, who knows what that has to do with it."

"Aren't demons supposed to get their powers at three in the morning?" Ashley asked. She shivered.

As grim as this conversation was, I liked it better than thinking about Dennis, who was still in his room. His body was in his room, but his soul was gone.

"Demons, ghosts...what difference does it make?" I said.

"A lot. Demons are evil and ghosts are just souls of dead people." Lea said it as if she had spent years studying it and was now presenting it in front of a class.

"*Only souls of dead people*. Do you hear how scary that sounds? And those things in this house seem pretty evil to me. They killed Dennis, they tried to kill me," I bounced back.

Lea fell silent. I shouldn't have said that.

"We don't know if it was those things," she mumbled a moment later.

"What do you mean by that?" I asked. My eyes got big. "You think one of us did that to him!"

"No! Of course not."

"Well, then what?"

"I just don't know anymore, okay?" Lea sobbed.

Kai, who had barely said a word, pulled Lea's head towards him. He rubbed her hair and soothed her, as she cried with great outbursts. This caused tears to roll down my cheeks again too.

"Maybe they're evil spirits," Kai suggested once everyone had calmed down.

Lea shrugged for the umpteenth time. That was something unique, because usually Lea knew everything. "I only know the stories. But what's real and what's made up? We can't rely on anything, only our own experiences."

A silence fell.

We waited in the dark for it to get light.

Chapter 19

Kai

And he then pulled the door behind him into the lock.

"Do you guys hear that?" Lea asked.

I jumped up and listened closely.

"I don't hear anything," Jill, who was extra wary, whispered.

Lea got up and walked over to the window. "Exactly. It's stopped raining. And look, the sun is shining!" Despite the plight, relief and joy resounded in her voice.

I got up and stood next to her, then looked outside. The sun was shining a beautiful glow over the mountains and the wet surroundings seemed to glisten. This image was so in contrast to what had happened to us. And with Dennis' death. A hollow feeling nestled in my lower abdomen as I thought of Dennis. My buddy. The one who had taken care of me so well when I had stayed put, the one who had introduced me to the three girls, one of whom would eventually become my girlfriend. I owed everything to Dennis. I took a deep breath. "We'll grab the necessary stuff and try a different way. Is there a ladder in the shed?" I asked. "Then we can climb over the fence."

"We can always try," Lea replied.

After everyone had put on normal clothes and

shoes - we did this without leaving anyone alone - we walked outside. The sun felt warm on my skin. Lea's hair took on a golden glow in the sun. It was beautiful, but not something we could enjoy right now. As the rest were already walking toward the gate, I said, "I'll be right back." I turned and walked toward the barn. Quick footsteps sounded behind me, I turned around.

"Not on your own," Lea said.

I smiled at her and together we walked on. On its own, the area around the house was beautiful to look at - Ashley's family owned a lot of land - but everything was outweighed by what had happened inside the house.

I quickly spotted the ladder in the shed next to the house. It was an old wooden ladder that was already a bit rickety. I wondered if someone came here regularly to maintain the surroundings. After all, it was full of trees, shrubs and plants. Without a gardener or a family member, this should be overgrown, right?

I grabbed the ladder and walked back to the rest with Lea. It was just long enough to see over the gate.

Jill immediately put a foot on the wooden ladder and climbed up. I held it tightly with both hands.

"Oh my god, my ring!" Ashley suddenly screeched, causing Jill to almost fall off the ladder in fright. Like a woman possessed, Ashley dove to the ground. Something glistened in her hand as she lifted it up and put it on her finger. She kissed the ring. "I've got you back." Ashley pressed her hand against her heart as if trying to give the object a hug. "So it was outside after all! That woman...ghost...spirit woman must have dropped it."

"How nice that you happened to see it," Lea said.

"Yes, how nice," Jill hummed.

I had almost forgotten that Ashley had lost her ring. Which was odd, because normally she wouldn't have stopped talking about something like that. My eyes turned to the top of the fence. I had to place a hand above my eyes to keep myself from being blinded by the sun. The sharp points established on top were far enough apart that I could see through them. The peeling green paint made the rust of the iron visible.

The fence was still a little bit too high for Jill. If she stretched out her hands, she could barely grasp the top.

"Can you see anything?" I asked.

"A little, but there are too many plants to look down decently. It's no use." She climbed down the ladder and wiped the paint residue sticking to her hands off on her pants.

"Now what?" Ashley asked.

I sighed. "Now we still have to get out of here. If necessary, we'll go on foot to find a town."

"One thing I don't get," Lea said suddenly. "Think about what happened yesterday and last night. They scare the crap out of us and try to kill us, which would make me think they want to see us flee. But then they don't let us leave. I don't get that."

She was right, it didn't make any sense at all. We were missing something. "It doesn't matter. We need to get out of here as soon as possible anyway," I said.

Jill looked up. "We have to climb over the fence via the ladder."

"Okay, who goes first?" Lea asked.

Ashley stepped forward. "Can I go? Sorry, but I'm so anxious to get out of this house."

Next to me I heard a soft growl from Jill, who clearly disagreed. To my great surprise, she kept her mouth shut.

I nodded, stood in front of the ladder and estimated the distance. "Do you think you're going to make it?"

"I'm not that small," Ashley said.

"But the fencing is high. Isn't it better if I go first?" I suggested. I wouldn't want her to fall.

"Why? Because you're a guy? I'm fine," Ashley hissed. "I just want to get out of here as soon as possible."

We all do, I thought, but I didn't say it. I raised my hands in defeat. "Okay, whatever you want."

Ashley climbed up the ladder. She was even smaller than Jill, so her hands only just reached the top. She had to climb up against the bars for a bit to reach the top. She managed to swing her leg up exactly between two pointed points. Groaning, jolting and bumping, she got both her legs on the other side of the fence. Slowly she let herself hang.

My heart sank at the sight. High above the ground she hung, dangling by her arms. If she landed wrong it could have dire consequences.

With one hand she grasped the steel, vertical bar that hung lower. She wouldn't find much grip on a smooth bar. Her second hand followed. And what I feared happened. She slid down.

She did not scream, gave no sign of fright. At one point we could no longer see her through the thick foliage of the ivy. We heard the thud that indicated she had landed on the ground.

"Ashley, are you okay?" Jill asked, who had sprinted to the fence.

"I'm fine," she replied.

I heaved a sigh of relief. The areas where the paint had initially peeled off were gone, which meant Ashley had shoved them off with her hands. Hopefully she hadn't sustained any injuries from that. The flakes could be treacherously sharp.

"Okay, who's next?" I asked.

Jill stepped forward. "I'll go."

For the second time today she climbed the ladder. Before she even managed to swing her legs over the railing, a strong wind came up. It hissed in my ears and blew under my shirt. It seemed as if the wind carried a puny laugh.

And then I heard it. Crack. In the middle of the ladder, out of nowhere, a large crack appeared.

"Jill!" I shouted. She managed to grab onto the top of the fence just in time before the ladder collapsed beneath her. I jumped backwards to avoid the falling ladder. "Hold on!"

"It's impossible! Those points are way too sharp!" And then she let go. The falling seemed to take ages, but in reality it took less than a second. All I could do was stretch out my arms, hoping to catch her properly.

Lea collided with me and together we caught her. The impact pulled me down by my arms and I landed on the ground with Jill. A creaking sound did not announce much good. Jill's face twisted in pain and she immediately grabbed her leg. Screamed. Like a rag doll she collapsed. She had still landed wrong.

"What happened?" I heard Ashley ask on the other side of the fence.

"She fell," Lea said. "Her hand slipped off the beam just as she grabbed it." She gulped. From her look, I could tell there was more to it. I gestured for her to tell me later. Whatever it was, Ashley needed to get help. Now not just to get us off this property, but for Jill as well. It didn't look good. She was wearing shorts, so her leg was visible. And under her skin, just below her right knee, was a sizable ball. I guessed that was bone.

Jill was screaming all kinds of unintelligible words and exclamations that I didn't want to repeat.

That caused me to jump into action immediately. I rushed over to her. "Can you stand?"

She shook her head, hissing and groaning.

"Ashley, get help right away!" I called to her.

Lea crouched down next to Jill and inspected her leg. "I'm not a doctor, but I can tell that's not good." Her chest heaved up and down.

I, too, had to recover from the shock.

Lea looked at the bright sun. "We need to sit in the shade. If we stay in the sun too long, we'll burn."

"Can we move her?" I asked. I think I had once read a piece about how you weren't allowed to move someone who had fallen or help them get up, they had to do that themselves, otherwise you could make the situation worse without knowing it.

"We'll leave her leg hanging."

"Do I have to go alone now?" Ashley cried.

"Yes, there's no way any of us are able to get over the fence with a broken ladder," Lea replied. "Besides, it's better for the two of us to take care of Jill."

On the other side, a sigh could be heard from Ashley. "Okay, I'll be back as soon as I can."

I heard the crunch of barren leaves on the ground, her footsteps getting further and further away from us. I couldn't remember how far we were from civilization. When I drove us here, we had travelled a long way through the woods and hadn't come across a house. Just a small town. It would be a while before Ashley would reach other people and also come back with help.

"Here..." I grabbed one of Jill's arms and slung it over my shoulders, then put my arm behind her back. On the other side, Lea did the same. I grabbed her left leg. In this way we carried her to a place where there were many trees, which gave us enough shade.

Chapter 20

Lea

Just keep breathing. Just keep living. Keep living to show the world who was the real culprit here.

"Careful," I said as we lowered Jill to the floor. She heaved a sigh of relief once she was seated.

"That leg needs to be kept high," Kai said.

I trusted his knowledge, some of which he had amassed through his volleyball training and injuries and some of which he had gained through his interest in the medical field.

My heart was still racing from what I had seen just before Jill fell. Could I tell now? While Jill was in so much pain? I didn't want to make it worse than it already was. Kai especially wouldn't appreciate it if I didn't say anything. I had already kept the kiss between Jill and Ashley from him, I couldn't do something like that again.

I looked around and saw a wide piece of tree root sticking out of the ground. With Kai's help I brought Jill to it, then laid her injured leg on it. The lump moved along under her skin.

She let herself fall backwards and rested her hands on her stomach. "I'm so nauseous," she groaned. With a reddened face, she pressed her jaws firmly together. A tear rolled down her cheek, not really sobbing.

Kai nodded. "Still, try to breathe in and out quietly through your stomach."

I gathered up the courage to tell my story, wanting to banish the image from my mind most of all. But it was stuck there, playing over and over again in my head, like a song on repeat.

"Listen," I finally brought out. "When you fell I saw..." I fell silent, not knowing how to explain it.

"What?" Kai insisted.

"I saw the face of a woman very vaguely. The sun was shining too bright to see the outline properly, as if her whole being was fading, but I'm sure I saw it. Right above Jill, near the top bar. It looked like she was causing Jill to miss and fall by just getting in between Jill's hands and the beam...hovering."

Kai ran his hands through his hair. "Shit. That spirit woman again?"

"Yes. What does this mean? Why is one so eager to keep us in and the other to get us out? Do they really want us gone or is their only purpose to scare us?" I asked. "It's so illogical. If they wanted us all dead, wouldn't we be long gone, instead of just Dennis? And why let Ashley out and not us?" I rattled.

"Maybe scaring us is part of their hunting ritual, before they kill us. And if one of their prey has escaped, they won't be happy," Jill said. Who seemed to have gathered all the strength she needed to get a sentence like that out of her mouth without letting pain shine through.

I saw my future go up in smoke. Our only hope was Ashley with outside help. Biting my lower lip, I sat down on the floor next to Jill. My eyes found Kai's brown ones. There were only three of us left and one of us was injured. The situation we were in was barely comprehensible. It was too ridiculous for words. How many times the thought had crossed my mind that this was something out of a movie or a book. In real life this did not exist. I wanted to believe in life after death, like a heaven. That had helped me for a long time after my grandmother died, the idea that maybe she was still with me, watching over me. I never cared that it might not exist. I was aware that it could be a fable, something out of faith, but if it helped me, why did it matter that I believed in it?

Besides, I had another question on my mind. If vengeful spirits actually roamed this house, would the afterlife, with its good souls, exist? As frightening as the first thought was, somewhere the confirmation that Grandma's soul could indeed be here gave me peace.

"I'll get some bandages from the first aid kit. Where did you leave them?" Kai asked. His words pulled me back to the present. "Then we can get ice and hold it in place on her leg and reinforce the rest."

"I think I brought that with me to the car. No, wait! It's still upstairs in the house." I cursed myself for having been so stupid as not to bring the first aid kit.

"Inside?" Kai looked with lips pressed together at the house that was far away from us.

"You don't have to go alone, I'll go with you," I said before I had given it much thought.

"What about Jill?"

"Oh, yes, of course. That won't do," I replied

dully. Shame ran to my cheeks. "But the house is so much more dangerous than here, right? I don't know, but..."

"Just go, please! I'd rather have some tools on my leg later than your discussion here. And can you bring a vest from my room? If I remember correctly it's on top of my bed," she spoke wearily. "I'm getting cold."

Goosebumps had appeared on her arms, but at the same time a drop of sweat rolled down her temple.

Kai breathed in and out deeply. "Okay, we'll be right back."

We walked to the house and straight upstairs as soon as we were inside. We didn't want to be inside a second longer than we had to.

"I put the first aid kit in the bathroom," I said.

I almost didn't dare look when I opened the bathroom door. What I saw took my breath away. The letters couldn't be clear enough. They looked like they were written with a shaky hand.

Shocked, I gasped for air. "Oh no."

"What?" I felt Kai's presence behind me.

"The mirror." I crept into the bathroom step after step, afraid that whoever or whatever had left the letters there would still be here. I looked around the room the moment I set foot across the threshold. Nothing. Just a normal bathroom. Wary, I stood right in front of the mirror. There was no condensation, so how could the letters be there? It looked like the word was written with a gray substance, but I had no idea what it could be. I raised my hand to the mirror. The line I made couldn't be seen. At least, not as clearly as the word that was there.

Help.

What was this supposed to mean? Was this a trap or did someone seriously need our help?

And then I noticed something crazy. There seemed to be space between the word and the side of the mirror I was looking at. As if it were a double-glazed window and someone had written something on it from the outside, while I was looking at it from the inside.

I ran a finger over the last letter. It didn't come off. It looked like this was written from the other side of the mirror.

"But how?" I whispered to myself. If the letters had been written via the other side of the mirror, what else could a ghost do? Suddenly I wanted to very much leave the room.

"Not a clue," Kai hummed next to me.

I swore that when I turned around, I saw a shadow in the corner of my eye. It was accompanied by a smell of fresh roses and ginger tea. I didn't want to know, I didn't want to see. With hurried steps I walked out the door, down the stairs.

My legs ran as fast as they could carry me. I heard Kai's footsteps behind me, but he was far away from me. Gasping and bumping, I dropped into the grass as I reached Jill.

"Hello, what's the matter with you?"

"Jill," Kai said when he had reached us. "Have you seen what's on our mirror?"

"What?" She frowned.

"On the mirror in our bathroom. Didn't you see

that?"

She shook her head. "I haven't been in the bathroom since last night. This morning I skipped brushing my teeth and showering too. We wanted to get out of there as soon as possible. I don't think any of us have been back there. So what is it?"

"It has 'help' written on it." Kai held up his hands and showed us a vest, a first aid kit, and the bag of ice I had put in the freezer when we arrived. Stupid. He had thought of all that and I had run away like a headless chicken.

We helped Jill put on the vest. Her whole body seemed cramped from the pain. I couldn't stand to see her like this.

"Help? Shit, man."

Kai wrapped the bandage tightly around the cloth and Jill's leg.

"Yo, careful!" Jill inhaled with a hissing noise and grabbed her upper leg with two hands.

"Sorry, Jill. You've got to bite through it," Kai said. Concentrating, he tied a tight knot in it. He checked that the bandage wasn't too tight or too loose, and when everything appeared to be in place, he stood up.

"You had seen a woman in the mirror last night, hadn't you?" I asked Jill.

She answered dazedly, "Yes. She had long black hair, an old-fashioned dress. I don't know. It was mostly the white eyes I saw." She shivered. "I didn't exactly pay attention to that, it scared me, you know. But, yeah, I think she's the same woman."

The gears in my head began to turn. Ashley had

seen a woman too, but at the time we hadn't believed her. And the one we had all seen outside...

It all added up. The descriptions, the events.

"We've got to get out of here. We have to find a way out," I said. We can't stay here any longer. Soon everything would happen again, one of us would be killed. And what if Ashley didn't come back in time? What if she didn't make it?

"How do you propose we do that?" Kai asked.

"We have to walk along the fencing to see if there's a hole somewhere. The grounds are huge and everything has been here for decades. It's hard for me to imagine that people have never tried to get in. There must be another exit somewhere."

"So you want to walk. What about Jill?"

I bit my lower lip. I didn't want to leave her alone again, but we had no other choice. "We have to if we want to get out of here. The sooner we get out, the better. And I hate to say it, but if we just sit here with the three of us, the chances of us dying are higher than if we actually try to find a way out and get away in time."

Kai looked from Jill to me and back again. "Jill, the choice is yours. You're the one who is going to stay here alone."

She closed her eyes, then breathed in and out deeply. "I will have to make do. I'll be fine. Give me something I can defend myself with. Lea's right, we need to get out of here as soon as possible."

Kai nodded, but reluctantly, and ran back to the house. It didn't feel right to me either to leave her alone, but we had no other choice. Jill couldn't walk.

"Hey, where are you going!" I called after him. He didn't answer. I decided to stay with Jill, I'm sure he knew what he was doing.

After less than a minute, he reappeared outside. Once he reached us, he handed Jill a large meat knife and a candlestick. "Here, be careful."

"Thank you. Now go." She gestured with her head in the direction of the woods behind us. A smile graced her face.

With a heavy heart, I walked away from her with Kai. A nasty feeling nestled in my lower abdomen.

Chapter 21

Kai

After all that, I had nothing left to live for. My life had been destroyed.

I heaved a deep sigh. We walked to the gate, the starting point of our search.

The area around the house itself was bare, as neat as if a gardener had maintained it, but closer to the fence, at the back of the property, it was wooded. No path ran through it, so we had to watch where we put our feet. Stinging nettles grew everywhere and thorny bushes blocked our way.

"This is never going to work. We can't even reach the fence through all the vegetation," Lea muttered. She hissed and pulled up her leg. A piece of skin had turned bright red. "Great, a nettle." She bent down, grabbed a couple of dandelions that grew there and rubbed them over the red spot after squeezing them.

"You okay?" I bent down and grabbed her lower leg to get a good look at it.

"Yeah. What about you?"

At first, I didn't understand what she was talking about until she pointed to my lower leg. There were small, red welts from thorn plants. The cuts were barely visible, but the drops of blood that seeped out and ran down my ankles were. I didn't feel much of it, though, other than some stinging.

"Don't worry, I'm a big boy."

She rolled her eyes. "You sure are big."

I swallowed my laughter. That comment could be interpreted in several ways.

We walked on quickly. The sooner we got out of this wooded area of dangerous plants, the better. I reached out my hand to her and helped her over an awkwardly lying tree stump. At last we reached the other end of the garden. As I had expected, there was no exit or secret gate here either.

Lea puffed.

I puffed and rubbed my forehead with my hand to wipe away the sweat.

"Okay, so this is the one corner of the grounds. Just a little while longer and we'll have covered it all," Lea said.

"Good idea. Then we can get back to Jill as soon as possible."

"How do you think she's holding up?"

I started walking again. "I hope she can hold on for a while."

"I mean...do you think she's still..." Her last word fell away hesitantly.

"Alive? I think so." I didn't want to make any empty promises, but somewhere I just knew Jill was safe. Besides, she was a strong girl. I wouldn't be surprised if even in this state she could knock someone off their feet. But now it wasn't just anyone. It wasn't even a someone. It was a something. And we had no idea what to do about it, how it worked. I had given her a candlestick and a huge knife, but who said that would help her? Suddenly I had a great urge to go back as soon as possible.

We travelled a long way in silence. It felt like a lull before the storm.

"What's that?" Lea asked. Ahead of us I saw something looming as soon as we left the woods.

I squeezed my eyes to slits against the sun. "No clue." It was roughly in our path, so we'd passed it anyway. Once we were in front of it and I could clearly see what it was, I shuddered all over my body.

"Ew, a cemetery." Lea sniffed.

Despite the fact that I didn't particularly like the idea, I walked toward the nature-worn headstones. These had not been cleaned for a long time. The letters had faded from erosion - but not so much that we couldn't read them anymore - cracks had formed in the stone from the changing weather and leaves were growing around them.

"Even better," I said, "a family cemetery. Look at it." I pointed to the headstones. "They all have the same last name."

Lea crouched beside me and looked with me. "How sad! Born in 1835 and died in the same year. There's a baby under here."

My blood froze.

"Oh no." Lea's mouth hung open. "Those baby noises we kept hearing. It wouldn't be..."

"That's too crazy for words, isn't it?" I swallowed and decided to read the next one. "Born in 1826 and died in 1835." And the next one. "Born in 1785, died in

1835. More children lie here. This whole row died in the year 1835. Those over there are from later." I pointed to the headstones that were a little further down. Then I pointed behind me. "And these are from much earlier." Lea joined me. "This is bizarre. Generations of family graves. They stop at 1916. I think that's when some of the family members moved and didn't want to be buried here. They all bear the same last name as Ashley, so these must be her ancestors."

Uncomfortably, we stared at the stones. A whole family died in the same year, that couldn't be a coincidence, could it?

"But if these are all Ashley's ancestors, who is she descended from?" Lea asked.

I shrugged. "Maybe an uncle or aunt of the residents, families were very large in those days. Does Ashley know this?"

"You'll have to ask her that," Lea replied. "Bah, this gives me the creeps." She rubbed her arms with her hands. Luckily these graves were far away from the house, otherwise I would have found it a lot more unpleasant too.

We had walked a whole round along the garden's fence, but without success. Everywhere the fence was overgrown with impenetrable plants and shrubs. The steel was too hard to break through, even if we had had a special saw. Nowhere was there a hole or an extra exit.

"Everything has been for nothing," Lea sighed. We walked in the direction of the house.

"Don't say that, Lea. We could've just as well have

found something." I put my arm around her and pulled her against me. Her desperation was palpable in the air.

"Let's go see Jill."

"Okay, come on," I panted. Despite the minute effort, I felt like I had run a marathon. We had still been walking fairly leisurely; my fitness level was really a lot better than that.

By the time we were within earshot of Jill, we heard nothing. That was either a very good or a very bad sign.

Then we heard a voice behind the bushes. "Yo, is that you guys?" Relief flooded over me when I heard her voice. She sounded weaker than before, but at least she was speaking.

She had placed the knife and candlestick on the ground beside her. Other than the fact that she was whiter than before and extra sweat beaded on her forehead, she looked surprisingly relaxed. The pain had to have gone to her head.

Jill looked at us hopefully.

"We haven't found anything that can get us out of this," I said regretfully.

"Nothing yet," Lea followed quickly. "We're going to search the house for things that can help us."

I tapped her shoulders gently. "Lea," I interrupted her. Had she gone mad?

"What? What else do you want to do? We can't just sit here waiting for Ashley. There must be something in the junk room. Anything." I hadn't said yes yet before she turned to Jill. "Anyway, do you need anything else?"

She nodded. "A glass of water would be nice. Good luck." It didn't sound wholehearted, but I didn't blame her.

Together with Lea, I walked to the house. "We have to be really quick. Who knows, her leg might get infected or something. She's in so much pain."

"Do you think I don't know that?" Lea hissed. "My worries about her are rising up to here." She raised her hand above her head to portray it.

"I know," I sighed.

It wasn't long before we were on the landing again. I didn't allow my gaze to fall to the end of the hallway, by Dennis' door. I was disgusted with the fact that his dead body was just lying there. In the middle of the room, nothing covering it. Waiting for someone to come and pick him up. *I'm sorry, Dennis*, I thought. *That we weren't there in time, that I couldn't save you.* The last thing I heard from him were his cries for help. He was calling for help.

"Are you coming?" Lea's words pulled me out of my thoughts. She had already opened the door to the junk room. "At least I found the box with the iron bars." She bent down and grabbed one of those things from the box. "But those are useless."

I began to dig into the nearest box, until my eye fell on a photograph lying next to the box. I picked it up and saw that it was yellowed. "Wow, this one must be really old," I whispered.

"What?" Lea saw what I had in my hands and crouched down next to me.

The people in the photo, probably an entire family,

were wearing clothes we didn't encounter these days. When I turned the photo over, I saw the year. "1834," I whispered. My gaze immediately shot to Lea and my thoughts went to the cemetery. What were the dates of death? All of them in 1835. Then these had to be those same people.

"There are names on here!" Lea shouted, who by now had gotten down on her knees and was flipping through the photos. She turned the picture my way so I could see it.

"Are those the same names as on the graves?"

"I believe so, but..."

"But what?"

"Well, there are four children and two adults in it, one of whom is a pregnant woman."

I drew my eyebrows together. "So?"

"On the graves we found one baby, four children's ages and one adult's age." She turned white.

Still I didn't understand what she was getting at with her explanation. "Say it already."

"One of the two adults has no grave. That person was never buried there. Haven't you ever read that the souls of those killed by violent death can't rest in peace? What if their spirits stayed here because one of the adults, I think one of the parents, killed everyone?"

My mouth fell open. In any other situation, I would have called her crazy now, but this made a lot of sense. I studied the picture I held in my hands again. "Oh, no." I swallowed. My heart hammered against my chest and I fell backwards.

"What?" Lea crawled over to me.

I pointed my finger at one of the two girls. "Her. She is the one I saw. She was hanging above our bed," I said with a trembling voice. "Her I saw outside the window too when I closed the shutters."

Lea snatched the picture from my hands. "And that woman, do you think she was the one we saw outside?"

I nodded.

She stood up, then pulled me to my feet. She ran down the stairs and I went after her. Once we got to Jill, we showed her the picture.

"Do you recognize anyone?"

Jill took the picture. It was trembling in her hand. "That woman...and that man." She breathed agitatedly. "Where did you get this?"

"I found it in the junk room. This picture was taken in 1834 and in the cemetery there was a whole family from 1835."

"Wait, what cemetery?" Panic grew on her face. We hadn't told her that yet, of course.

"While searching, we stumbled upon a family cemetery. And as Kai just said, there were a lot of graves from 1835 in there. We think they died in an unnatural way and their souls can't find rest. They are still in this house."

"Not only are they still in the house, they want revenge," Jill said. Her voice cracked. "They killed Dennis, they're scaring us. Why would that be?"

Revenge seemed the logical explanation.

"Something doesn't add up. I can't explain it, but this doesn't feel like just revenge. It feels like much more than that." Lea slumped to the ground.

"So Ashley's great-great-grandparents are haunting this house?" Jill asked.

"I don't know anymore."

Lea ignored my comment, far too absorbed in her own thinking. "There's a grave missing. There must be something about that."

"Do you think whoever it was killed the family?" I asked cautiously.

"I don't know," she replied.

I, too, decided to take a seat on the ground. "And what did she mean by 'help'? You don't write that for no reason, do you?"

"Then it seems to me that she needs help. The woman wrote this on the mirror, I saw her that night, and as soon as you walk into the bathroom, you'll see that written," Jill remarked.

"Or it's a ruse," I said, "is she trying to trap us?"

Lea crossed her arms. "What kind of trap? Think about it. What would she want to achieve with the word 'help'?"

"Help, that's what she wants." Jill put the picture down beside her.

"But how?" Lea asked. Her arms fell limply by her sides. "This is driving me crazy."

"None of it matters. All that matters is that we can get out of here as soon as possible."

Jill tried to move herself very carefully. "What if we can't leave until we've helped her?"

I looked up. Jill was right. What I was about to say sounded so incredibly stupid to me. It could also make the situation worse. Did we really have no other choice? If we sat here and waited, there was a good chance we would end up like Dennis. Every time I thought about him, it felt like a deep black hole formed in my stomach. An emptiness. Besides, we couldn't get off this property. This could help us. "We can ask her."

Chapter 22

Jill

My legs turned into jelly and I began to sweat profusely.

"And how did you plan on doing that?" I raised my eyebrows at him as I wrapped my vest closer around me. At this point, I didn't know if the chills were from the pain or from the conversation.

"A séance," Kai said.

"And how would you like to do that?" Lea repeated my question. She stood up and placed her hands at her sides. "Why should we?"

"We've seen enough movies." Kai shrugged. "Some of it must be true, right?"

"And you want to rely on what they say in those bad horror movies? You're crazy." Lea shook her head. "Sorry, but I'll pass. If it even works, and I say if it does, we all know the nasty consequences of relying on what happens in movies. I don't want that. I want to get rid of the problems, not bring them upon us." She threw her hands in the air in desperation.

On this front, I agreed with Lea. If the movies taught us anything at all, it was that all the real problems started after spirits were summoned. Or demons. On the other hand...who knows, maybe all the trouble would stop as soon as we helped the woman who wrote that message on the mirror. And then we had to figure out what she needed our help for. Or maybe there were fewer problems if we did what they said.

"We have to do this," I agreed with Kai. "That's the only way we can possibly get out of this house."

"Yeah, or die in it," she snapped at me. "Just like Dennis."

I flinched and tears sprang to my eyes at the thought of Dennis. I wasn't used to this cattiness from her. Neither was Kai by the looks of it, for he caressed her back thoughtfully. At first, Lea didn't seem to need that. She tried to wrestle herself out of his grasp, but he wouldn't let her. Finally, she surrendered to his good intentions and leaned against him.

"Lea, we're not going to die. I'll make sure nothing happens to us," he murmured.

How could you make such a promise when you didn't know what was coming? What the outcome was? Still, it seemed to calm Lea.

"It's worth a try. After all, she said we couldn't leave until she wanted us to, and maybe she'll let us go if we help her," she finally muttered. "But I'll kill you if we die." It was meant to be a joke to make the situation more light-hearted, but it had the opposite effect. Making a situation better with jokes was clearly not her strong point, it was Dennis'. If only he were here. "How do we handle this?" she then asked.

Kai scratched the back of his neck. "Dark room, candles and summoning?" He sounded anything but confident.

I rolled my eyes. "That's exactly what we're going to do. Now we just have to actually get there." I nodded in the direction of the house.

"Will it work if we lift you?" Kai studied my leg.

"It'll just have to do."

Lea and Kai bent down, then lifted me, careful not to strain my injured leg. As if communicating telepathically with each other, they carried me effortlessly to the house. The closer we got to the building, the harder my heart began to beat. For them, this was the umpteenth time they had gone back into the house; I had not been there since we had left it after Dennis' death...

"One of you has to close the shutters down here and the other one has to go and look for candles," I said after they had lowered me onto the living room couch.

"Why do we need candles anyway?" Lea asked.

"Light for us? Or fire as an element of nature that enhances summoning? I don't know. But if you want to be able to see, you'll have to find candles," I replied.

She sighed and turned to look for them, muttering, "Are there any candles at all in this cursed house?" before disappearing from my sight.

Sitting like this on the couch I felt incredibly useless and at the same time the pain came back. With no distractions, I was alone with my thoughts and those thoughts were currently focused on my knee. I didn't dare look at it yet, but by the looks Lea and Kai gave me I knew enough. The signals sent to my brain told me that I needed to get to the hospital as soon as possible.

The living room grew darker and darker as Kai

closed all the shutters one by one.

"Do you know how exactly a séance like this works?" I asked him.

He glanced over his shoulder and then continued closing the shutters. "Not really, to be honest. But don't tell Lea. She's already worrying so much."

"And rightly so." I snorted. "We don't even know if it works, but it could go so terribly wrong."

He drew his eyebrows together. "Don't say that."

Just then, Lea came back into the living room. "Miraculously, there was a drawer full of candles in the kitchen," she said. In her hand she had candles and a matchbox. The long, yellowish candles looked like they had been lit several times and were covered in dust.

Kai was just closing the last shutter.

"Now what?" I asked.

"We'll have to sit in a circle while holding hands..."

I interrupted him. "Really, that sounds so silly."

"I'm just imitating the movies," Kai defended himself. "So, circle. The candles between us. And then summon." He looked at me. "I also feel ridiculous saying this out loud."

"Okay, here we go." They moved the table my leg was on to the left - so my leg was still laying on the edge - and Lea put the candles on the floor next to it. Despite the fact that my leg barely moved in the process, I felt the pain it caused. Kai took a seat on the table and Lea on the wooden floor. She took the matchbook from her pocket and lit the candles a moment later.

The lit candles shone an ominous glow through the

room and shadows played on the walls. Their faces were illuminated in such a way that I could only see a few parts of them. Their cheekbones were accentuated and their eyes glinted in the dark, reflecting the light of the candles.

"Who will speak?" Lea asked. She looked at us all anxiously.

"Me," Kai said. "I came up with the whole idea, so I'll be the one to call on her." He extended his hands to us. His hand felt clammy and warm, while Lea's was ice cold.

"Can't we say something like 'we bring light and love' or something?" Lea asked.

"Why?" Kai raised an eyebrow.

"So we don't attract bad things."

I wobbled back and forth uncomfortably. "Lea, what we are going to conjure up in this house is bad."

"Of course I know what we are going to summon is bad, but that doesn't mean we can't take precautions."

Kai cleared his throat. "Then we will begin now." He gave Lea a reassuring squeeze of her hand.

My heart was beating at lightning speed and I was so focused on my surroundings and what was about to happen that the pain faded into the background.

"We come in light and love," Kai began, "we call to the one who wrote the message on the mirror. We know you want to tell us something."

For seconds we waited. My eyes closed, hands in those of Lea and Kai. And nothing happened. Just when we asked, they didn't feel the need to let us know they were there. It was eerily quiet. I didn't know what would be worse; that we wouldn't hear anything or that something would happen.

"We know you need help. We want to know what you expect from us," Kai tried again.

Suddenly the sound of the crackling flame increased violently and my face grew warmer. Startled, we opened our eyes and let go of each other's hands. The fire raised itself high. I wanted to flinch, but my leg made that impossible. The air filled with static energy.

A breeze slid along my skin, causing goosebumps and the hairs on my arms to stand up. Then I felt a long, bony finger brush along my neck.

"Jill," I heard close to my ear. It was a rasping, weak female voice. I breathed hurriedly. What was she going to do to me? I squeezed my eyes stiffly shut. I didn't want this, make it go away. The oppressive feeling, which I didn't realize was there at first, slid off my shoulders. From left to right. As if they were walking past me. Judging by the movements of their heads, the same thing happened to Lea and Kai.

Somewhere we heard a bang that shook the house to its foundations. The fire from the candles played up even more and suddenly a white light shone in the doorway from the living room to the hallway.

I broke out in a cold sweat.

There she stood.

The woman I had seen in the mirror. The woman we had all seen outside. In the doorway she stood dead still looking at us. Only her eyes slid over us. She had her hands folded in front of her. Her dress was draped gracefully around her body in shades of gray, black and white. Her cheeks were sunken and her eyes were as white as I could remember. I could see right through her, see the wall behind her.

Kai jumped up and positioned himself in front of Lea, while she remained seated as if frozen. I could do nothing but stay in my spot, staring at the woman all three of us saw.

A scent of roses and ginger spread through the room, tantalizing my senses. A laughing baby sounded at the end of the hallway.

Kai half-turned, watching the woman and Lea at the same time. He sank through his knees and grabbed Lea's arms. With his help, she stood up. He held her tightly as he stared at the doorway.

My breathing quickened and my hands trembled. It was the middle of the day, but in here - despite the candles - it was so dark you'd almost think night had long since set in.

Her face remained impassive as she slowly raised her arm. She pointed to something diagonally beside her.

Strangely, I no longer felt threatened by her presence. Maybe it was the scent that had managed to calm me, maybe it was her aura. There seemed to be an aura of reassurance coming from her, as if she were trying to tell us without words that we could trust her. It had been different in the bathroom, but I realized that had been more due to my own fear than the fact that it was her.

"Look," her feathery voice sounded. The sound

was carried along by the breeze that died down shortly after. It had something compelling, something stern, yet I was no longer afraid.

Kai and Lea looked at each other briefly. Then their eyes fell on me, helpless on the couch.

"Why?" Kai asked. A slight tremor was audible in his voice.

"Come," the woman whispered.

"I don't think she says more than one word at a time. Maybe more is too hard for her, takes too much strength," I guessed.

The woman's gaze focused on me for a moment, I thought I saw her nod.

"Okay." Lea took a step forward, looking at Kai and me.

"Go with her," I told Kai. "I'll be fine." How many times had I said this sentence today? Swallowing, I turned my gaze to the woman, who by now had moved a few steps to the side, as if she wanted to go ahead of them.

Lea took another step. Kai walked behind her. Before I knew it, they were out of my sight.

Despite the fact that I could no longer see them, I felt the presence of an entity. Probably the woman's. It had to be. The space felt charged and an invisible force pressed down on me.

Just as I heard a door slam in the hallway and Lea's scream, a powerful hand clamped around my mouth.

Chapter 23

Lea

"You will never be found. People will think you killed your family. That you are the culprit. Which is true, of course, but sometimes people need an extra push to believe that."

As we stood in front of the basement door, the woman gestured for us to go in. Kai stopped me as I took the first step. "Wait, you don't know what could happen."

"All I know is that we've been startled in this house all along, that Dennis is dead, and all the horror won't stop until we do something about it. I think this is it. We have to follow her."

From the corner of his eye, Kai studied the woman. How I would have liked to know what was going on in that head of his.

It wasn't necessarily her presence that scared me, but the idea that ghosts really existed. That she was right next to me. I was still hoping to wake up from a bad dream at any moment.

I opened the basement door and took a step across the threshold. I expected Kai to follow right behind me, but instead the door slammed shut behind me. Startled, I turned around. "Hey!" I rattled the doorknob. The thing moved up and down, but I couldn't pull the door open any further. "Kai!"

On the other side of the door, I heard him calling

my name, then he inhaled with a sharp sound. That was what caused me to stop pulling, punching, and yelling. I listened intently to what it was that startled Kai. It became deadly quiet around me. I no longer heard the birds chirping outside, I no longer heard Kai. Only my own breathing and the creaking of the ceiling sounded in the room. I pressed my ear against the door. The rough wood scraped across my cheek.

"Kai?" I asked softly.

I heard him breathe, but it took him a while to say anything. "Lea, be careful."

"What for?" My voice was shaking, as was my whole body. I was alone in a dark basement, locked in, and my boyfriend was on the other side of the door, warning me of something I couldn't see. Should I beware of the female spirit or was there something else that was in this dark space?

Far away, I heard stumbling, murmuring, and a choked cry.

"Jill!" Kai yelled.

"What is it?"

"There's something wrong with Jill," he said.

I put two flat hands against the door and rested my head between them against the wood. I had made the decision quickly. "Go to her, I'll be fine."

"But..."

"Go! She's the one who's hurt and needs help, not me." I immediately regretted these words. I didn't want to be left alone. I needed him. But Jill needed his help more than I did. Given our experiences with doors and gates suddenly not opening, there was no getting around it.

Moments later, I caught on to what Kai was trying to warn me about. A while after his footsteps died away, a hand came through the wood of the door.

I flinched. What I had overlooked was that this was the door to the basement, which meant there was a staircase leading down behind me. Just as I was about to lose my balance on the top step, I managed to grab hold of the banister.

The hand was followed by an arm, then successively a leg, a face and the rest of her body appeared. Although the light could not reach this basement, I could see her clearly. The glow around her made her visible to me.

She didn't do anything, just looked at me, as she had done a moment ago.

I stared back, clasping my hands tightly around the banister.

She extended her hand to me, but before she could grab me - if she could at all - she turned around in a flash. It looked like that rapid movement was interspersed with slow motion. She literally flickered.

The door was flung open with a bang and very briefly I saw the shape of a man standing there, but the door didn't stay open long enough for me to get a good look at what he looked like. The woman pointed at the door and it slammed shut again. Then it jumped open a crack, moved toward the lock again, and the door was thwarted by another force. Yet there was no doubt that that was the man from the picture.

They were fighting over the door. Open or shut.

This was my chance. I stormed forward, grabbed the door handle and pulled. I had wanted to help her, but her locking me in was not the deal. Now I wanted to get out of here as quickly as possible. I stood right next to her, but forced myself not to think about that. The door opened further and further, almost I had regained my freedom. I had to escape. Until an invisible force pulled at me. It was as if my whole being was being grabbed and thrown away. For a moment it felt like I was flying. Around me was nothing but air and darkness. Until I landed on the stairs with a hard crash. The edges of the steps stabbed into my back, legs, stomach, head as I rolled down. There seemed to be no end in sight. I didn't even have time to produce a cry for help. When the rolling stopped and I landed with a thump on the floor at the bottom of the stairs, the air was knocked out of my lungs. Squealing, I sucked in a gulp of air.

"Kai." It was nothing more than a rasping whisper. He would never be able to hear me.

I tried to clear my head and groaned as I moved my limbs. I pushed myself off the floor with my hands and slowly but surely managed to get to my knees. Facing the stairs and with my hands on the bottom step, I looked up.

It looked like there was a real fight going on. Where I had first seen the woman on this side of the door, there were now two additional shapes standing beside her. I blinked rapidly, trying to get the image clear. Two young boys. And by the looks of them, they were helping the woman. Their mother, said a little voice in my head.

What was going on here? Was I unconscious? Was I in a coma and was this a dream?

While the two little boys remained standing by the door, the woman floated down the stairs. I crawled to the side and pressed myself against the wall so she could pass me and not walk right through me. I had no desire to experience what that felt like. She towered high above me as she looked down on me. I swallowed the lump in my throat.

"Esmeralda," she said in a whisper.

My bottom lip quivered as I tried to thrust the words out. "What, no, my...my name is Lea. But...you already knew that," I said as I thought about her saying my name in the living room.

She shook her head. "Esmeralda."

"Esmeralda? Is that your...name then?"

She nodded.

Was she really speaking or was I hearing her voice in my head? Because her lips didn't move.

I didn't even have to ask what she wanted, because with her arm she made it clear that I should follow her. "Quickly," it sounded.

My gaze fell on something shiny next to me on the floor. My phone. Of course, I always had that with me just in case. I saw that the screen was cracked, but I still managed to unlock it. That was of later concern. Quickly I turned on my flashlight. I used the wall to lift myself up.

Staggering on my legs, I followed her. My head felt cloudy, as if a fog had risen that silenced my thoughts.

Like a mindless creature, I did as she said.

My flashlight shone through the room. I recognized this from somewhere. A flash of my dream shot through my mind. How I was in someone else's body, how I was forced to walk forward from behind. But this was different. This didn't feel forced. And I was myself. Could she have been the cause of that dream?

After passing a lot of old junk, Esmeralda stopped in front of a closet that stood against the wall.

This image, too, I remembered. Only now did I realize that the man I had seen in my dream was the man in the picture, who was now standing upstairs by the door.

The image of how that man moved the cabinet came up. As if someone had planted that there. I looked at Esmeralda. It was her. She was showing me these things.

Her snow-white eyes looked at me compellingly.

I should be scared, but I wasn't. Was I being stupid?

As I walked to the closet, she stepped away from it. I placed my hands against the side of the object, tried to estimate how heavy it was, and pushed. The cabinet moved a few inches. It wasn't enough. I didn't have enough strength to slide the cabinet far enough to get through the opening.

Before I knew it, I muttered, "If you can keep all those doors closed, can you at least help me with this closet?" The blood drained from my face as I realized what I had just said out loud. Out of the corner of my eye, I looked in her direction.

All she did was shake her head and she pointed to the door. Somehow I immediately understood what she meant. From here she was still trying to keep the door closed upstairs.

I still wasn't sure if that was good or bad. She was keeping me here, the man wanted the door open. What were his motivations? With whom was I safest?

Finally, I threw my full weight into the fray. I pounded against the cabinet and again when the first attempt fell short. The cabinet tilted forward slowly at first, before it landed on the floor with a smack. The wood banged on the floor and the things inside rang loudly. Behind it was a dark hole. When I shone my flashlight into it, I discovered a corridor whose sides and top were made of earth.

Esmeralda preceded me.

As soon as I walked through the hole, I noticed that it was significantly colder here. The hallway was wet and didn't seem like a place you'd liked to come. I could tell by the odd thickness of the walls that this had been dug out by hand. In some places there were wooden beams that were supposed to hold the earth back. The earth had been flattened everywhere to keep it firmly in place. It looked like this had been sitting there for hundreds of years, unnoticed and sealed off from the world. There was a sharp smell of the mold settling in my nose.

She led me further down the corridor. It was one long, straight road with no obstacles. It looked like something out of an Indiana Jones movie. Spiders crawled along the walls, on the floor. I accidentally stepped on them, they were so big they creaked under my shoes.

My stomach turned over. My fear of spiders was not at all convenient for me at this moment. I didn't mind the worms wriggling through the earth as much.

Esmeralda's stature hovered above the ground, as if gravity didn't apply to her. Somehow it made sense, for she had no body to be held to the ground. This was her soul. Could I feel her if I touched her? Earlier I had felt fingers, we had all felt things or been touched, but were they in control? Could they decide when we could feel them, when they could physically touch something? It was a peculiar thought.

A few minutes later, I felt a breeze brush along my arms. There was a draft. Which meant there was another exit somewhere.

The end of the corridor was coming into view. Or, well, the end...there was a door. It looked like a wooden square had been erected in the middle of the corridor, blocking the passage. And the door had been built messily between them.

Esmeralda disappeared through that door. Just through it. As if there was no matter.

I moved my hand toward the door. What I would find would surely be no fun. Too late. I had to go through now. She had written 'help' on the mirror, she had led me here. Maybe I was actually helping her and this wasn't a ruse. Besides, other than throwing me down the stairs, she hadn't hurt me. It was obvious she wanted me here. Hopefully I wouldn't regret my decision.

The door opened surprisingly smoothly. A musty smell overtook me and immediately I put my hand over my nose and mouth. I shone my flashlight into the room. It was not large. In this room the walls and ceiling consisted entirely of wooden boards and beams, but it looked messy. Probably this too was homemade. Against the wall at the back were several wooden crates stacked on top of each other, which served as stairs. I squinted upward. There was something that looked like a hatch. As if this were the entrance to an air raid shelter, only this room was not an air raid shelter, as there was no stock of food.

I shone the flashlight to all corners of the room. My breath caught in my throat and my blood instantly turned ice cold. My phone slipped between my fingers, landed on the floor and suddenly I was enveloped in complete darkness.

"Oh my..." Nothing more came out of my mouth.

This was the first time in my life I had seen a human skeleton. It sat there as if someone had sat there and died like that, after which it had been preserved for centuries. There was no flesh left on it, yet it was crawling with critters.

I bent down to pick up my phone.

Esmeralda floated over to the skeleton, stood next to it and bowed her head.

And then it dawned on me.

"Is that you?" I asked incredulously.

She nodded.

A fit of sadness overtook me. "Was this what you

needed our help for?"

Another affirmative nod, after which it seemed as if her stream of thoughts entered my head.

"You wanted your body to be found," I observed. "Is it true then that spirits stay on earth because there is something that keeps them here? Is that in your case that your body was never found?"

A simple head movement told me enough.

My fear disappeared. I knew exactly what her goal was, as if she were sending me those words. She wanted people to know that her body was here. She just wanted peace. She wanted the truth to come to light. I frowned. What truth? Suddenly my thoughts were broken off. Or the connection of her thoughts to mine was interrupted. I couldn't receive anything anymore.

"I'm going to tell the others about this," I said more to myself than to her. "Don't worry, your body won't be here forever."

I didn't feel like making my way back through the cold, wet corridor only to end up at the door where the other ghosts were probably still standing. What were they still doing on earth? That question ran through my head as I looked at the hatch above my head.

Chapter 24

Kai

He took his hand from Aaltje's mouth and stood up.

Before I even reached the living room, I heard Jill's choked cries. For that small stretch, I ran even faster. On the way, I came across an iron candle holder. On reflex, and for lack of anything better, I took the thing. I only needed a second to take in what was happening.

Behind Jill stood a young girl, I estimated her to be no older than twelve. Her hair fanned out around her head like a wreath. A cold sweat broke out as I recognized her as the girl who hung from the ceiling above me last night. Her hand was over Jill's mouth. My eyes flashed around the room, but there was no one, or nothing, else.

Because of the fact that Jill was struggling, I could tell that the girl could physically touch her. This time her touch didn't go through Jill like it did me last night.

"Let go of her!" I called out what first came to mind.

Her head shot up, in my direction. A jet of deep red blood seeped from her mouth and traced a line down the side of her chin. As the corners of her mouth moved upward in a smile, I saw that her teeth were red. Black veins ran down her face to her neck and disappeared under her dress. Her eyes hinted at the craziness that was inside her. It radiated from her and penetrated under my skin. I felt trapped in her gaze.

She still hadn't let go of Jill.

I pressed my jaws firmly together and stepped toward her with large strides. The candle holder whizzed through the air as I lashed out with it. I expected to hit her, to recoil, to make her flinch. But the iron went right through her and she dissolved into nothingness. A shiver crept up through my hands the moment they went through her.

I tried to keep my cool as I took care of Jill, who was lying on the couch gasping for breath.

"You okay?" I put a hand on her shoulder to let her know I was with her.

She coughed. 'Yeah, no. I don't know. What was all that about?"

Other than the fact that her skin had gotten whiter after the fall anyway, it now looked as white as snow. Including the moisture. Sweat droplets beaded on her forehead and ran down her temples. Now that I saw her like this, all the medical knowledge I had amassed while watching hospital series came to the surface. And all I could think of was that the sweating, the shivering, her skin gone white, and the warm feeling were not good signs.

"Do you have a candlestick in your hand right now?" she asked dazedly.

"Yes. I had to have something, right?"

Jill reached for the knife and another candlestick lying next to her and held them up to me. "You're not going to tell me that those fiction stories about ghosts not being able to stand iron are true, are you? Because otherwise I'll keep these with me." She tried to push herself upright. Her leg slowly slid off the table.

"Wow, what do you think you're doing?"

"You're crazy if you expect me to sit here. I'll put up with this pain no matter what, as long as we can get out of here."

"But Lea is stuck in the basement. With that ghost." The image of a lifeless Lea shot through my mind. If I happened to find her like that...

"That woman?"

I nodded. It felt like my throat was being squeezed shut.

"How did that happen?" she wanted to know.

"The woman slammed the door before I could enter after Lea and a moment later the woman followed her. Who knows what she'll do to her." Doomsday scenarios kept flooding into my head. I shook my head in an attempt to dispel them. "I'll open the shutters. Hopefully it's also true that ghosts are less powerful in daylight." Like a man possessed, I ran around the room, throwing open every shutter. I didn't bother to fasten them properly to the hooks hanging in the outside wall. "Okay, now I'm going to go get Lea."

"Get salt," Jill said.

That took me off guard. "What?"

"What are the odds that a circle of salt will help keep the ghosts out? Ever seen Supernatural? We can at least try."

"But it's already bright inside, so first Lea. Stay put."

She crossed her arms and rolled her eyes. "Seriously? Like I have many options on my own."

I ignored her comment and made my way to the hallway. I didn't get very far. As soon as I walked into the hallway and my gaze fell on the basement door, I took another step back into the living room. In front of the door stood another apparition. A man. The father. In the second I saw him, I could have looked right through him and it became clear to me that he was trying to open the door. But why? Which side was he on? Was he trying to help Lea and go against the woman or did he have a completely different plan? Just to be sure, I backed away.

So how was I going to get to Lea? Who knew what this tall, slender man would do if I disturbed him at the door. I didn't want to take the risk of getting hurt, too, because then Lea would have no use for me at all. I had to live to help her. So I sneaked into the kitchen. How much sense was there in sneaking? Without any information about how the real spirit world worked, I didn't know what the best thing was to do. What they could and couldn't do, what they heard and didn't hear. Could they read minds?

In the kitchen, I soon found a can of salt. Just regular table salt. Thank you for your orderliness, Lea.

"What should I do with it?" I asked as soon as I entered the living room.

If she was at all surprised that I was standing here again and not having Lea with me, she didn't show it. "Sprinkle it in a circle, make sure it's a tight circle. If all goes well they can't get through that. So we have to be inside of it."

I did as she said. I was careful with the salt, because this was our only bus and the circle was getting big, since Jill had to stay seated so I had to sprinkle around the couch. With each step I took it felt like someone was moving along behind me. I cast several glances over my shoulder, but each time no one was standing. Once the whole circle was there, I plopped down on the couch next to Jill. Now we could do nothing but wait, hope for the best. The uncertainty of Lea's situation consumed me inside. Every part of my body wanted to spring into action, but I couldn't.

Lea. I didn't hear her scream, she didn't knock against the door anymore. All I heard was the sound of the door slamming open and shut. Not knowing what was going on was terrible. And the waiting was driving me crazy. My leg twitched up and down uncontrollably and I tapped my teeth with my fingers.

"Yo, stop that," Jill hissed.

"Sorry."

"Wait..." Jill placed an index finger in front of her lips. "You hear that?"

I listened. Jill and I looked straight at each other as we focused our hearing on our surroundings.

Keep your cool, I thought. *Panic never solves a situation.* Again I got the feeling that someone was right behind me. This time it felt more real, more alive. As if my body was sending a signal to my brain that this time it wasn't my imagination.

Jill's eyes flashed to me and fixated on something behind me. I saw her swallow. My fear reflected in her eyes.

"What do you see?"

"She's standing there, outside the circle. But it's so bright in here. How..."

"Don't think about that," I said. "This is not a movie. This is reality." Even my breathing I tried to make inaudible. It didn't make that much sense, because it was clear she could see us. "But the circle helps?" I wanted to know.

"I think so." She spoke as if her throat was being squeezed.

"Okay, that's good." Actually, I didn't want to turn around, but I had to. That way I could keep an eye on her. Slowly I stood up and turned around. Her face was much closer to mine than I had expected.

With her head tilted, she stood there. Blood dripped from her chin onto her white-gray dress. Her dress still had a red stain in the middle of her stomach.

"She can't get in," Jill whispered. More to herself than to me.

My gaze slid to the girl's feet, which were sheathed in a pair of old-looking shoes. They were indeed standing still right in front of the salt.

A gust of wind rushed through the house. That one made Jill's hair blow up, as did the girl's hair. But it did something else that we absolutely could not be dealing with right now. Slowly the salt came out of its place and an opening was created. The gust of wind was her doing, I was sure of it.

She took a shaky step forward. She moved forward as if the bones in her body could break at any moment.

I reached out to her with the iron candlestick, but I missed, didn't dare get too close. I was afraid. Terrified of what she might do to us. Of the fact that we might suffer the same fate as Dennis. Ashley would soon come back to find all her friends dead.

Step by step the girl snuck up on us.

"Hit her!" Jill cried in a panic. Using her hands and arms, she moved herself backwards across the couch, away from the girl.

I lashed out once more. This time I did hit her. She disappeared. That did not reassure me. She could appear anywhere. Right in front of me, right behind me. In a place where I wouldn't be fast enough to defend myself or Jill. I spun around my axis in circles.

An icy sensation shot through my arm. I looked down. A livid white hand was gripping me. Her nails were pressing into my skin, making welts. A drop of blood came up. She squeezed so hard I couldn't tear my arm free. It felt like several ice cubes were pressing directly into my skin. She moved her hand in such a way that my arm had to go along with it. That movement, the angle my arm ended up at, and her nails drilling sharply into my skin cut off enough of the feeling to my fingers to weaken them. The candle holder slipped from my hand.

I flinched, but because she was holding my arm, I was forced to take a step back. In her direction.

Her eternal smile frightened me, froze my blood.

I was so absorbed in the moment that I didn't realize Jill had rolled herself off the couch until I saw movement below me. I looked out of the corner of my eye and saw her handing me the knife.

Somehow I had to distract the girl. She was holding me, which meant we were now in physical contact. That was it. With my left hand I reached out and punched her in the face. A loud snap sounded. Her head had turned a little more than a quarter turn and seemed to be stuck at an unnatural angle. A piece of bone protruded from her neck. Her grip on my arm slackened.

At the same time, I looked at Jill, who was lying at my feet. She grabbed the candlestick as she thrust the knife into my hands. Immediately I thrust it through the girl's body. Skin-to-skin contact was okay, but as soon as the iron touched her body, it went through air and she was gone.

I sank to my knees, put my arms under Jill's armpits and pulled her up. She groaned.

"Just hang on," I instructed her. "We have to get out of this house."

Together we stumbled toward the hallway. That was the only way we could get out. The only problem was that the father's translucent apparition was still at the basement door, which we couldn't avoid.

I supported Jill; she was the only one who had two hands free to touch him. As soon as Jill slammed the candlestick through him, his figure disappeared and the door slammed shut.

"Lea!" With the hand I was using to hold the knife, I fumbled at the latch. Because I had to support Jill, I couldn't use my full strength. There was no movement in the door. My girlfriend. I had to get to her. I couldn't leave her to her own devices.

"Kai, watch out!" Jill cried. I turned myself and her around. Jill lashed out with the candle holder and the girl who had crept up behind us disappeared again. Suddenly the corridor was eerily quiet, almost deserted. Only the charged energy that still lingered told me that we were not really alone.

"We have to go out now and hope they don't follow us."

"But Lea..."

"Kai, we have to get out of this house alive if we want to save Lea. We're no good to her if we die."

I took one last look at the basement door before I moved to the door in pain and dragged Jill out of the house with me.

Chapter 25

Jill

There was nothing I could do.

Outside, the sun was higher in the sky than it had been a moment ago, but new clouds blocked out this morning's bright sun.

When I rolled off the couch, so much adrenaline had shot through my body that I didn't feel the pain in my leg. Now, however, it came back. And more severe than before. The stiches that plagued my body felt like knives constantly being pulled in and out.

I held on to Kai as I hobbled along. "Where do you want to go?" I groaned with my jaws clamped together. Every time one of those shooting pains shot through my leg, the muscles in my jaw automatically tightened and my breath caught in my throat.

"Not a clue. Away from this house, that's for sure. As far back in the garden as possible."

"Where the graveyards are?" Yeah, because that was really where I wanted to be at the moment.

"Yes, I think so."

"What about the other corner of the garden?" There had to be a better place than the final resting place of those who were currently haunting us.

Kai shook his head. "There's nothing there, just tightly packed bushes and nettles, impassable."

As more and more clouds gathered, the warmth of the sun disappeared. It felt damp, muggy. My vision was getting blurrier. I had to hold on. Meanwhile, the cloth of ice - which had already begun to melt due to my body heat - slipped under the carefully applied bandage.

Kai was running faster and faster and I was having trouble keeping up with him with my leg. He dragged me behind him, which forced me to lean on my aching leg.

"Yo, slow down," I hissed. "We'll get there." A little way down the road I saw headstones sticking out of the ground.

"Sorry, you okay?"

Stiches shot from my knee throughout my body. "Yeah," I lied. The closer we got to the cemetery, the weirder I found it. "You know what's bizarre? Didn't they used to be very religious? Then you'd think they'd want to be buried in the church cemetery, rather than some random spot in the garden," I realized.

"Not everyone was religious. Some had other traditions, I think. I don't think it was entirely unusual for there to be family graves on private land before that time. I can't be sure. Besides, centuries-old family traditions are more important to some."

I snorted. "Family traditions are sometimes nothing more than peer pressure from your deceased ancestors." I knew so many people who didn't really want to carry on their traditions, but because it was 'the way it was supposed to be' they had to.

Panting, we stumbled forward. The moment we

passed the stones, Kai gently let go of me. I slowly sank to the ground and finally sat down in the grass. Breathing was hard for me. As if my throat was being squeezed and an elephant was dancing on my chest at the same time.

Kai stood there for a while, turning his head from side to side, scanning the surroundings. His gaze fell on the house several times, where Lea was still standing.

"And now?" I asked.

"Now we wait for Ashley to come back with help and hope that whatever is in the house doesn't come out until the sun has at least set. I need to get back as soon as possible to see if I can get to Lea yet. Whether they'll let me near her yet." He kicked at a loose rock. "Do you hear what I'm saying? 'Whether they'll let me near Lea. Those...things...are in control and there's nothing we can do about it. We're stuck." Hopelessly, he placed his hands on his neck and turned his head to the sky.

"You can't go to Lea just yet." As I said that, his face was like thunder, but after he realized that as well, his expression softened. "Ashley will probably be back soon. She's been gone all morning. It will take a couple of hours for her to reach the nearest village and then they have to get here with cars and help." For myself, I tried to put everything in order. Her return could take longer than I thought. "They somehow break open the fence and we're out of here."

"But what if Lea is still trapped, or if they do something to us? I don't think she has ghosthunters with her. Besides, would she even know the way? Who knows, she might get lost or something bad might happen or...or the ghosts might be chasing her out there too." He waved the knife around, causing me to almost automatically reach for the candlestick I had placed on the floor next to me.

I drew my eyebrows together. "Kai, calm down. You're starting to rattle off like Lea. So far, the knowledge of the movies has helped us. If we are to believe them, ghosts are usually tied to a place. A place where either their bodies lie, or where they have great emotional value. And since their bodies are here," I nodded in the direction of the headstones diagonally behind us, "I think there's a good chance they can't get off the grounds." My knee throbbed terribly and I bit my lip. With my hand I pressed around the throbbing area, trying to ease the pain.

"That's why they want to keep us in, why they've sealed everything off. Because they can't get to us outside of this fence," Kai supplemented my thoughts.

I nodded. "We just have to make sure we can get out of here."

A groan rolled across my lips. I fervently wished the adrenaline would shoot through my body again, so I wouldn't have to feel everything every time I moved my leg even a millimeter.

I cursed the spirit that had dropped me. Thanks to her, I was left with a broken leg and was useless, a burden. Kai would have been much better off with Lea, or even Ashley. Or Dennis... I felt tears stinging behind my eyes.

"I can never make it right," I sobbed.

Kai crouched down next to me. "Make what right?"

"That I kissed his girlfriend. That with Ashley. I can never apologize again. He's dead and we had a fight." My heart split in two at the realization. I wanted him to know that I was sorry, so very sorry. I wanted to talk it out with him, joke with him again if he would ever forgive me. But none of that was possible anymore. For the rest of my life I would walk around with the knowledge that I had hurt my best friend and had never been able to let him know how sorry I really was.

Kai sighed and put a hand on my shoulder.

Next to me I heard rustling. With my head heated from the pain and my vision blurry from tears, I looked at the leaves moving up and down a few feet next to me. A few leaves came up and shifted, as if a huge beast was moving underneath them. I crawled backwards as best I could, bumping into Kai's leg.

"What is it?"

I pointed.

He looked.

We waited.

Kai still had the knife in his hands, I had my candlestick and those were the only things we could defend ourselves with.

The leaves stewed in the air and a piece of wood came up. Followed by a hand sticking up above the earth. The hand was covered in mud and grappled around the hole it had created. *Are there damn zombies crawling out of the ground now*, I thought. The way the hand moved and its soft shapes reminded me of a woman's hand.

"Wait a minute..." Kai took a few steps in that direction.

"Kai, don't be stupid!" I watched as he bent over the hole and, in my opinion, got way too close to the grasping hand. He dropped to his knees and grabbed the hand.

My meal from last night came up. With a look full of disgust, I watched. That changed when I saw his happy face, then a smile also appeared on my face the moment I saw a mud-stained Lea.

Kai pulled her up from the hole and immediately took her into his arms. He buried his face in her neck. It seemed like I could literally see the pressure fall off his shoulders; he relaxed and his shoulders sagged. Lea pressed herself against him, letting out a deep sigh. He apparently didn't care that she was covered in mud and smelled awful.

"Are you all right? Sorry, I should have done more, fought harder to get you out. But I didn't know how," Kai said. He pulled back from the embrace and framed her face with his large hands.

Lea nodded. "It's all right, Kai, I'm fine. I'm just a little shaken up."

Kai blew out a long sigh. He rubbed her upper arms and pressed a kiss to her forehead, which Lea received with a small smile.

I quickly wiped the tears from my cheeks before Lea noticed me.

"Jill!" She rushed over to me. "Are you okay? How

did you manage to come all the way here?"

"He was supporting me. It was painful." I squeezed out a non-meaningful smile.

"What happened down there?" Kai asked.

Lea looked at the hole. "I have to show you that. That was her goal, for people to know."

"Know what?" This time the question came from me.

"You'll see in a moment, it's important that several people see it, so you have to come down with me."

Kai and I exchanged a look. She sounded like a lunatic who was speaking gibberish and in riddles.

"Wait." I shuffled on my butt in their direction. "First of all, I don't trust whatever is in there, whatever it is, and secondly...I can't go through that hole with my leg, I have to stay here."

"We're not leaving you alone," Lea immediately said.

"You have to. Besides, I have the iron candlestick with me, we know it works. It's also light outside, so they probably won't come here."

"But it's already cloudy, it's getting darker," Kai worriedly said.

I sighed and for the umpteenth time I urgently said, "I'll be fine."

Kai looked down through the hole. "Off you go then."

Lea, who had already lowered herself, went first, and Kai quickly followed. What was I to think of a random hole in a random spot in the garden? The musty smoke rising from it hit my face as I sat down closer to the hole.

"Jill?" I heard Kai's voice from the darkness below me. "Stay there, we can just see you from here."

For a moment I was eager to lower myself into the hole too, so I wouldn't be left alone. My leg made that impossible, though, so I hung my head above it. Two beams of light filled the room, probably their flashlights. Boxes were stacked just below the opening, serving as a sort of staircase. This was clearly well thought out. And it was also such a long way from the house, how had they managed it? A tunnel?

"There." Lea shone the flashlight from her phone towards the corner of the room. I just couldn't see what was there.

Kai coughed. "A skeleton?"

"A what?" I exclaimed. Had I heard that correctly? There was a skeleton in a room that was somehow connected to the house? I couldn't contain my curiosity. "What does it look like?"

"Um, it's an old skeleton. Just bone, there's no meat left on it, it's in the corner of the room," Kai hesitantly replied.

I shuddered. Maybe I should learn to control my curiosity after all. Then again, there were things in life I didn't necessarily need to know. Like this.

The combination of the smell that rose from below and the vivid description that was now in my head really made my stomach contents rise to the surface. I half-turned my body and threw up in the grass. Quickly I wiped my mouth with the back of my hand.

A tremor went through my body. At first, I

thought it was just me and due to the condition with my leg, but soon I realized the house was shaking on its foundations.

"Too late!" roared a voice through the house.

I had never heard such a volume before in my life. And that voice, so infused with anger and deep-seated emotions. The power behind it made his voice cut through my head.

Down below, Lea lost her balance and landed on the ground. Kai I could not see from this position.

A fierce sting ripped through my scalp. I flew backwards a few feet and landed on the earth with a thud. The air was knocked out of my lungs.

A crackling sound filled my ears. I didn't even have a chance to look up before the hatch slammed shut with a bang. The shaking stopped. My attention was caught by an unnatural cloud that gathered just above the house. It was smoke. My eyes grew large. The house was on fire!

Only then did I look at the hatch. Two girls were standing in front of it, slowly coming my way. A sob welled up in the back of my throat. My gaze slid to the candlestick, which was behind them and which I could not reach with any effort.

Chapter 26

Lea

A flame was brewing inside me, a primal force, more powerful than I had ever felt.

Above us, crackles sounded. I didn't have a chance to look up before the hatch closed with a bang. The shaking stopped.

"Fuck!" I exclaimed.

"Jill's alone!" Kai braced himself against the wall and ran toward the crates that served as a sort of staircase. He pushed against the hatch. There was no movement. "Jill!" He hit the wood with his flat hand until it began to vibrate.

"Kai, leave it. It's no use. It's the same as the gate and the basement door. We can't get those open unless they want them to," I sighed defeated.

"Shit." He climbed down from the crates. "Then we'll try at the basement door." He wasn't done with this yet.

"Okay." I placed my hands around my mouth and yelled, "Jill, if you can hear us, we're going to the basement door."

Except for the sound of the wind that had picked up, I heard nothing. Surely nothing had happened to her? If anything, there was nothing I could do about it. What I could do about it was get us to safety, make sure we got out of the house as soon as possible and rejoin Jill.

I rubbed my face with my hands, then balled them into fists. Renewed fighting spirit flowed through my body. "Come with me."

I led us down the hallway. My haste caused my elbows to rub against the walls of earth several times. The hallway was barely wide enough for two people.

I slowed my stride when a peculiar smell reached me. I sniffed. "Do you smell that too?"

"Smoke," Kai said. His eyes grew large. "Quick! There's a fire in the house."

We ran as fast as we could to the basement. It was pretty hard in a hallway lit only by a flashlight that constantly moved up and down as we ran. I was a sprinter, not a long distance runner. My lungs began to burn and the lactic acid in my muscles increased. Kai had less of a problem with it, running ahead of me. I followed the light of his flashlight. We were lucky that this was one straight corridor and not a labyrinth.

Eventually we emerged into the cluttered basement. I watched as smoke was already coming through under the door. It wasn't too much.

"They're gone!" I called out. The boys were no longer at the door. I sprinted up the basement stairs, dodging other junk.

"Lea, wait!" I heard Kai come after me, but he stopped when I gave a tug on the door and it flew open in one go.

The heat overwhelmed me. A cloud of smoke filled the room, my eyes immediately began to sting because of it. Quickly I grabbed the collar of my shirt and pulled it up to hold it in front of my mouth and nose. We were absolutely not allowed to breathe in smoke. At least, as little as possible. I gestured to Kai to follow my lead, which he did. Holding his shirt in front of his nose and mouth, he walked up the stairs.

No sane person would walk into a blaze, but staying here was not an option either. This was our only way out.

"Why aren't they fighting over the door anymore?" Kai asked.

"Because that's our only way out, and we're walking toward our deaths. If we go through that door, we'll end up in the fire. They're very keen to keep the skeleton hidden," I shouted above the sound of crackling flames. I coughed through the smoke that caused a stinging sensation in my airways. "They've done everything they can to prevent us from finding her, it seems like this is their last solution to keep her secret!"

The flames outside the basement were already licking at the ceiling, blocking our only way out.

I'm going to burn alive, was the first thought that floated through my head. This was how my life would end, swallowed up by a blaze in a cursed house. My body would never be found, or it would be so unrecognizably charred that teeth impressions would have to be taken to figure out who was who. And no one would know that Esmeralda's body lay here.

The spirits had gotten their way. Esmeralda's body would not be found; we would not be able to escape to pass the news on. But there was one advantage to having the house go up in flames. That was that the spirits perished along with the house. They, too, were signing on for their own eternal resting place. How I was so sure of this knowledge was beyond me, but a little voice in my head whispered it to me. Thoughts that were not my own flooded into my head, letting me know things that were unknown to me.

We stood at the top of the basement stairs and watched as the hallway in front of us was swallowed up in thick smoke. A red glow shone through the room. The heat scorched the house and left scorch marks. My lungs felt thick and full from the unconsciously inhaled smoke. They stung worse and worse. My eyes began to water. I gathered more dust from my shirt to stuff in front of my nose and mouth.

I was nearing despair the moment a white light loomed in front of us. Through the thick smoke I could see her.

"Esmeralda," I coughed.

"Who?" Kai asked.

"That's her name." My voice was smothered by the fabric I held in front of my mouth and almost didn't rise above the deafening sound of the fire.

At the spot where Esmeralda stood, the smoke scattered. The flames seemed to avoid her. Her hair moved around her face as if the wind were playing with it. She walked toward us. The fear I felt during the first time I saw her had completely dissipated. I knew what she wanted, what her only goal was. It had never been her intention to injure us or frighten us, all she wanted was help. And we had offered her that help. That was why she was now trying to get us out of this house in one piece. At least, those were the words and images that suddenly shot through my head. They were not my own thoughts. It seemed as if Esmeralda had planted them there, as if this was her way of communicating without words.

Within seconds she stood right in front of us, preventing the flames and smoke from reaching us as well. Esmeralda remained unaffected. She turned around so that her back was almost glued to my stomach. And I knew what that meant.

"She wants us to follow her," I informed Kai.

"You're crazy. You're not walking into the fire, are you? Lea..." A coughing fit interrupted his contradiction.

"What do you want to do? Soon you'll be burned alive, but not Esmeralda. Trust me, she'll help us," I assured him.

He nodded and followed me as I trailed Esmeralda.

All around us we heard the crackling, saw how the walls and ceiling were turning black. High flames made the opening to the living room inaccessible, as did the stairs leading upstairs. For a moment, all the things I had left behind shot through my mind. The books that meant so much to me, clothes I was attached to and... Dennis. He was still up there. His body would burn to ashes. Tears sprang to my eyes. It took all the strength I had in me to get my mind off it, to realize that there was nothing I could do about it. How had the fire started in the first place? I had no doubt that this was the work of the other spirits, but how had they managed it?

Esmeralda kept the flames from hitting us with a force we couldn't see as she floated toward the front door.

But there was a problem. The door was blocked by a tall figure, accompanied by two smaller ones. The father and two daughters. My heart rate shot up and instinctively I almost wanted to run away.

Esmeralda stopped in her stride for a moment. She seemed to hesitate. Something changed in her posture. Her black hair blew up even higher. She stretched out her arms. A deafening screech sounded as she threw herself forward.

Bewildered, I remained standing, watching the scene. Because of the smoke and the shirt I was holding to my face, everything happened in a blur. As if I wasn't really there.

Esmeralda flew at the man, who dissolved into nothingness with her, only to reappear a few feet away. The flames around us, however, came no closer. Somehow Esmeralda managed to keep the fire away from us. The two were engaged in a fierce fight. It didn't look like a physical fight, more like a mental game. Whose powers were stronger? Who was overcoming the other?

The two girls were watching us. One had blood coming out of her mouth running down her chin and dress. A blood stain was on her dress, at the level of her stomach. I recognized her as the one Kai had described.

The other girl had a deep red streak running the width of her throat with blood pouring out quickly.

This was our chance. While she distracted her husband, we had to get past these two girls to get outside.

I looked at Kai, who was looking at the knife in his hand. Only now did I see that he had the thing in his hands. How long had he been carrying that around?

Kai could defend himself, but I had no iron. I had nothing to protect myself with.

The two girls were standing in front of us. They looked up at me. At first, it seemed like they would stay like that, until suddenly one grabbed my arm. Even before she could tighten her grip, I jerked free and Kai thrust the knife into her side. At least, that was the intention, but it went right through her and she disappeared into thin air. Her sister, who was a little taller, didn't seem to care. With a quick pull, the iron went right through her as well.

Kai was soon behind me as I put my hand on the doorknob. A hissing sound came from my hand as I touched the doorknob. I pulled back. The heat in the room had made that latch glow. My palm was slowly turning red.

"Lea, are you okay?"

Yeah. I only burned my hand on a doorknob that had become red-hot because the house was set on fire by evil spirits. I'm fine, I thought irritably. But I nodded and bit through the throbbing pain.

"The knife! Cut off a piece of your pants."

Kai immediately did as I said. Quickly he put the

knife in his pants and he yanked on them, loosening the fabric. I wrapped my hand in the fabric and moved it to the doorknob again. This time it was there as an extra layer and the heat didn't affect my skin. I glanced back. Only this bit by the front door, where we stood, had not yet gone up in flames. Esmeralda and her husband were still fighting.

Suddenly the man looked up. His head shot our way and his eyes flashed to my hand on the doorknob. "No!" he roared. The air trembled from it.

It startled me so badly that I pulled the door open with one pull. But before I could take a step across the threshold, I was yanked hard by my hair. I stumbled backwards and landed on the floor, my face only inches from the blaze. Above me hung the head of one of the girls. She was looking at me intensely, her eyes widened and focused on one point, holding me in place with unprecedented strength. I looked to my right, where Kai was in exactly the same position. He was fighting and trying to stab the girl sitting on him with the knife.

I focused on the girl above me again, doing everything I could to struggle out from under her. However, there was more keeping me in place than just her physical strength. This was not a fair game, but I had known that from the start. Blood seeped from her mouth as she smiled at me. Her hand moved from my wrist, which she held, to my throat. She squeezed it tightly. My lungs prickled from the smoke and burned from the lack of oxygen. Black spots appeared before my eyes. Everything around me became blurry. The sound of the crackling flames faded into the background and Kai was only a vague blur. The signals were no longer transmitted to my brain, couldn't make it a coherent image. My legs convulsed, my body shook uncontrollably. And despite all that, only one thought came to mind: *you killed Dennis. Your hands were around his neck.*

Suddenly I gasped for air. The pressure was gone and smoke drifted in. The spots before my eyes slowly disappeared and I could distinguish two figures. One was the girl. I focused my gaze. First I saw shorts, then his shirt and I could discern blond curls.

The figure threw the girl into the flames and turned to me. His familiar, friendly eyes looked at me with concern.

"Dennis," I squeaked. It was really him. He was here. "Dennis," I repeated.

Slowly, I stood up. His eyes sparkled, seemed anything but sad. He even seemed...happy? I walked toward him, my arms spread to embrace him, but a shadow appeared behind him.

"Watch out!" I called out to Dennis. But it was too late. The man hit him and Dennis disappeared into thin air.

"No!" I shrieked.

"Lea!" Kai ran towards me, I was glad to see that he had managed to break free.

Esmeralda, along with the shapes that had appeared, attacked the man. Two young boys. They fended him off as I slowly stumbled backwards and Kai grabbed me by the arm. He dragged me with him without mercy, out of the house.

"No, wait! Dennis!" I cried desperately.

Stumbling, we ran across the grass, until my body gave up. My lungs felt too heavy to take in enough air and my legs were shaking. I sank to my knees and rolled onto my back. The front door was wide open, and there I saw them. Father and daughters fighting to get to us, mother and sons holding them back. An additional apparition with blond curls appeared. He pushed one of the girls aside.

"Dennis?" Kai's voice broke.

"It's Dennis," I whispered. I crawled over to Kai and pressed myself against him. He grabbed me tightly.

Even the spirits in the house were no longer untouchable by the flames. As if Esmeralda had allowed it, the fire came closer. Closer and closer, until I heard screaming. First the husband and daughters went up in flames screaming and roaring. Then the little boys could not escape it either, but they seemed to be at peace with it, until the fire reached Esmeralda. Dennis turned around in the doorway, took one last look at us, and smiled.

"Thank you," I whispered as warm tears rolled down my cheeks.

He nodded as a sign that he had heard me, before he too was swallowed up by the fire. The fire consumed the last remnants of their souls.

The screams died away and suddenly a very heavy burden fell from my shoulders. Coughing and coughing I hoisted myself up until I was on my knees.

"Are you okay?" Kai asked with a face drawn with pain. His face was smeared with ash, I don't think mine looked much better.

"Yes, are you?" I didn't know how to make sense of anything. He nodded in response.

"Dennis, he..."

"He saved us." And somewhere I knew it was alright, that he had found his peace. His last act was saving us from a horrible death.

Chapter 27

Lea

Until the darkness fully embraced me.

Oh my god, Jill, was my next thought. We had last seen her at the hatch. But because of the distance and the thick smoke rising from the house, combined with the heat of the flames making my eyes water, I couldn't see anything.

Panting, I got to my feet. I stumbled a few feet in that direction. "Jill!" I coughed and grabbed at my neck, which still didn't seem to let enough oxygen through.

"Lea, don't." Kai had quickly come up behind me and grabbed my arm, then immediately pulled me with him, a few steps back. "We're still too close to the house." His voice sounded hoarse. "Who knows how much smoke we've already breathed in inside; we can't afford to breathe in anymore."

"But we can't leave Jill behind!" Indignant, I looked at him.

"Of course not, but it doesn't do Jill any good either if we put ourselves in danger for her. Besides, if she's still in the spot where we left her, she's far enough away from the fire," he reasoned.

"Jill has a broken leg, Kai. That hatch didn't slam shut on its own. We don't know what happened to her, so what if she too…"

He pulled me towards him and grabbed my face with both hands. "I refuse to think like that. Jill had the candlestick; she knows how to defend herself. All we have to do is get out of here."

I stumbled after him to the gate. A strange feeling settled in my lower abdomen and tingled through my body. What we were doing was not right. Still, Kai was right. Jill had nothing to gain by us killing ourselves. Nevertheless, every cell in my body screamed at me to turn around and look for her.

The closer we got to the gate, the further the crackling sound of the burning house subsided. And as if the universe was in our good graces, I heard sirens. They were already very close, but too late. The house was already completely consumed by flames. Along with Dennis. His family would have no body to say goodbye to. Only a pile of ashes. My heart split in two.

Once we reached the gate, Kai pulled the latch. Miraculously, the gate opened. It seemed there was no resistance at all.

"Of course," he whispered hoarsely, "the one who was keeping the gate closed has just burst into flames. She has no control over it anymore."

We had discovered Esmeralda's body, we were free, which meant we could pass on that information and she would get the rest she deserved.

The sirens grew louder by the second and suddenly different colors flashed in my face. Vehicles were driving in our direction. Police, fire and ambulance. Ashley had pulled it off! She had to have kept quiet about the ghosts, or they would never have believed her, let alone turned up. Had she only told them about Dennis' death?

My knees softened with relief and I let myself fall into the grass. Kai, on the other hand, stood more erect than he had a moment ago and waved eagerly at the people in the vehicles. A small cough escaped him.

The first to get into my view was a fireman. I couldn't imagine what he must be seeing now. A house ablaze and two teenagers who looked like they had crawled down a chimney.

"Come with me," he shouted in our direction, he had a Belgian accent. "You have to get out of here." The fireman dropped to his knees and grabbed my arms, then pulled me up.

I held on to him tightly. It felt like my legs might give way at any moment. Suddenly I was shaking all over my body.

"Our friend, she's still somewhere on the grounds!" I shouted. I was shocked at how hysterical I sounded. Only when I felt something warm run down my cheek did I realize I was crying.

The man nodded. "Where?"

"We last saw her behind the house, quite a distance from it." A coughing fit escaped me. "Please, you have to find her!" I said when the coughing had finally stopped.

"Okay, go to the ambulance. They'll take care of you."

Before I had a chance to walk there myself, two EMTs appeared in front of me. One took me along while supporting me, while the other took care of Kai.

We were both put in different ambulance trucks and I couldn't see him anymore.

"Kai, where is he?" My voice sounded increasingly hoarse.

"Don't worry, girl. He'll be well looked after."

My breathing quickened, I wanted to see him! I wanted him with me.

Firefighters, paramedics and police were running up and down the streets. I wasn't sane enough to fully grasp what they were all doing. All I could see was them running into the yard, toward the house and past it.

The adrenaline subsided. The pain in my lungs, hand, head and whole body became more and more palpable. I got an oxygen mask shoved over my face. Everything happened in a blur. I had no sense of time and didn't realize what was happening to me. I was barely able to answer the questions that were being fired at me.

Was I in pain there? How was my breathing? Did I feel like I was getting enough oxygen? Dizzy? Who was I? What had happened? That last question was asked by the police officer who had come to stand beside me. I was in an ambulance with an oxygen mask on my face, I had stumbled out of the house not even a few minutes ago - not yet burned alive - and he came and asked me this question already? I couldn't even sort out the events myself.

I couldn't see Kai, I didn't know where Jill was and Dennis was in that house, his spirit had saved us.

"Where's Ashley?" I asked. My voice was partially muffled by the oxygen mask I had on.

The policeman frowned. "You mean the girl who warned us?"

I nodded.

"Is it smart to bring her in?" He asked the question not to me, but to the ambulance crew. Still, I nodded my head fast.

"As long as she doesn't get too worked up, it's not a problem. We've examined her. She is out of danger, but will still need to go to the hospital for further monitoring."

Not getting too worked up? Those people were crazy.

The policeman gestured and called out to someone outside my field of vision. A few moments later, I heard rapid footsteps. The blond hair was the first thing I saw. Ashley ran between the cars in my direction, followed by a policeman. As soon as she saw me, she quickened her pace.

Without regard for others or the equipment on and around me, she flew around my neck. She pressed me tightly against her and I wrapped my arms around her.

"Sorry, I'm so sorry. I wish I had been quicker, what happened?"

Relief spread through my body. It felt like a fine tingle that started in my chest, worked its way to my stomach and then to the rest of my body. For a moment, I felt lightheaded and the worries disappeared. Not only had she managed to get so much help, she looked unharmed, apart from a few scratches on her arms and legs.

"Ash, it's okay," I whispered.

"Easy, don't talk too much," the ambulance attendant spoke to me sternly.

I followed her advice and didn't say anything back.

This time it was tears of relief and joy that made tracks in the ashes on my face.

"Where's Kai?" Ashley asked after she let go of me.

I looked at the EMT, who pointed to an ambulance a little further away.

"How is he doing?"

"I don't know, but I think he is in the same condition as your friend here."

"And Jill? Where's Jill?"

I stared at my feet. The worst possible scenarios filled my head.

"No, is she..."

"I don't know," I brought out, because at the same time I didn't want to assume the worst. My emotions fluctuated between remaining calm and panicking, between relief, joy and intense sadness.

My gaze fell on the house, which was being extinguished by the fire department. But it was too late. All the wood was already corroded and with a lot of roaring, parts of the house collapsed. Everything swallowed up, along with our belongings and Dennis. From here, I didn't know where Dennis' body was, nor did I see him fall among the rubble. I squeezed my eyes shut, not wanting to think about those images.

As I sat here like this, I realized how little value material possessions had. I was alive. We were alive. That was all that mattered.

I was rudely pulled from my thoughts by ambulance workers who suddenly ran past us to the gate. I got up quickly. A little too quickly, because I immediately saw stars. The woman from the ambulance spoke sternly to me and supported me, as I had absolutely no intention of sitting down again.

Further away, police officers and firemen approached. Between them hung a body. Her brown hair dangled in front of her eyes and her clothes were soaked with blood. The red color contrasted sharply with her light skin.

Jill. She seemed to be struggling to stand on her feet, but she was walking along, which told me she was still alive.

I placed a hand on my heart, Ashley squeezed my other hand. We couldn't get to her, weren't allowed to get in the way of the EMTs while they rendered the necessary assistance.

"Ashley, keep an eye on Jill, please. I'm fine."

Ashley nodded and disappeared between the cars.

I looked around and saw that the area had been cordoned off with red and white ribbons.

Everyone around me was busy, having a task, and I just sat there. "Can I please go see my boyfriend?" I almost begged, but I had to be with Kai.

"In a minute," she kindly said.

I nodded. That was already better than before.

My eyes didn't know where to look. I looked at the emergency workers running by, stared at the house that was already almost completely extinguished. How long had I been sitting here?

"Come on, let's go," said the ambulance attendant. She carefully placed me on the stretcher in the car and closed the doors. She stayed with me.

"Wait, I was allowed to go to my boyfriend!"

"You'll see him later at the hospital."

My breathing quickened. I knew I was safe with these professional people, but I had lost control.

"Try to stay calm. He's going to be fine. They're riding behind us."

"What about Jill?" I asked with a trembling voice.

"I'm not allowed to say anything about that."

My head plopped back on the headboard. If she could say that Kai was fine, but not tell me how Jill was doing, it could only mean something serious. We couldn't lose another person. And where was Ashley? How did she get to the hospital? And what would happen to Dennis' body? Our car was right next to the house and had not been left undamaged.

After we told the police our names, they called our parents. It would be a few more hours before they got here, but the fact that they were coming was a relief. I was monitored in the hospital for a while, but it was soon clear that I was out of danger. I might suffer from sensitive airways or shortness of breath later. I was free to move around the hospital and visit my friends. So now we were all sitting around Jill's bed.

Ashley had ridden with the ambulance that had transported Jill to the hospital. She told me that she hadn't left Jill's side for a second. I was told by Ashley that they had operated immediately on Jill's fracture in her leg and stitched up her cuts. We had no idea what had happened to Jill when we were inside and she was left behind. She had looked like she had been badly beaten.

Also, Ashley said it had taken her hours to find a village. There she had been so desperate that she had signaled a passing car and it had stopped for her.

"The driver had given me a lift into town. I know it's stupid to just get in with a stranger, but at that moment I saw no other choice. At the police station I told them that Dennis had been killed by strangers - I could hardly say that ghosts had done it - and that you were locked up. They feared for our lives because you were with dangerous people and immediately drove to the house. The clouds of smoke could be seen from afar and they had no doubt that it was that house that was on fire, so the fire department was immediately called in. It also turned out that there was already a fire truck nearby, so we got there quickly."

"Thank you so much, Ashley. Without you, we might not be sitting here right now. Or at least not as healthy as we are now," I said and gave her an intimate embrace. I had been annoyed with her more times than I liked, but the nagging girl seemed to have disappeared.

Kai heaved a sigh and put his arms around us. Jill had tears running down her cheeks. We sat in her hospital room, which she had to herself, and talked to each other about what had happened. As traumatic as these events were, I had to talk about them.

"It was Dennis, he saved us." With wide eyes, Ashley and Jill looked at me. "I thought I was dead when the girl attacked me, but there he was. He was standing in the doorway looking at us when we were outside and it was like he was saying goodbye to us." Warm tears rolled down my cheeks at the thought of our best friend who managed to save us even in death. "He saved my life." I sobbed.

The rest remained silent.

The image of Dennis smiling at us shot past each time. I consoled myself with the thought that he had finally found peace.

"And what happened to you, Jill?" She had to stay in her bed and moved carefully so that her stitches didn't pop open.

She shook her head. "It's all so vague. Two girls slammed the hatch and attacked me. I had the candlestick, but it was out of reach. One of the girls saw it and made sure I couldn't reach it. They came at me and I couldn't get away." She looked at us with tearful eyes. "You know those dreams where you're being chased and you can't run away? That you get stuck behind something on the ground or constantly fall over? That's how I felt in that situation. Only this time it wasn't a dream." She swallowed. "They were hitting me and stabbing me - with what I don't know - I managed to fend them off from time to time, but because of that fucking leg of mine, I couldn't fight back. And suddenly they disappeared into thin air... If that hadn't happened, I wouldn't be lying here."

At that realization, I exhaled shakily. Then we had lost another loved one.

"Could it be because the house was on fire? If

ghosts attach themselves to a place and it disappears, would they disappear too? Or maybe it was because we had found Esmeralda's skeleton and escaped. If their goal was to keep her body hidden, they should also have no reason to be in that place anymore if they failed, right?" Kai asked.

"It could be, but we'll never know for sure," I sighed. "I personally think they were summoned by their father to stop us from leaving the house."

Ashley smiled at us with watery eyes and looked ahead with a distant look on her face.

Heavy footsteps entered the room and I looked up. A female and a male police officer stood in the doorway. They looked imposing in their blue uniforms with weapons and items they used in their service.

"We have news about your friend, Dennis," the female officer said.

I held my breath. I was curious to hear what she had to say.

"We found his body. When his family gets here, they'll decide what's going to happen to it."

"What's going to happen to him. He's still a person," Ashley hummed.

The policewoman nodded and apologized.

I balled my hands into fists, my nails pricking my palm. My burnt palm had been treated with a few ointments and burn plasters. It had blisters and red spots with peeling pieces of skin on it.

Earlier, there had been other police officers. They had asked us for our statements, which went a lot better when my voice wasn't hoarse from the smoke. For a while I had been furious, because they insinuated that we were reckless teenagers who had set the house on fire. The fire department had found out that the fire had started in the kitchen, near the stove.

Of course I told the cops the truth, no matter how stupid it sounded. But this was better than telling them that there had been real people who had killed Dennis and were trying to harm us, because otherwise they would be looking for someone who didn't exist. I told them that we had found Esmeralda's body in a secret passage under the house. I had also described where the hatch in the backyard was located. They had indeed found that, as well as her skeleton. To our good fortune, the earth of the secret passage was so cold that the fire could not continue, and so that room, and Esmeralda, had remained untouched. They promised me that they would investigate the family that had lived there before and what had happened to that family, but I had little faith that it would lead to anything. At least they believed the part about the skeleton. But the ghosts, all the other events, they wrote off as hallucinations. Those were the unimaginative brains of adults, people who didn't dare think of the possibility. I was probably also lucky that the police did not see us as suspects despite our crazy stories. After all, we were the only ones in the house, along with Dennis.

It took a while, but eventually I let it rest. It was Kai who had managed that.

Now I just wanted to go home. To lie in my own bed, to fall into the familiar arms of my parents.

What exactly had happened in that house with

Esmeralda and her family, so many years ago, we would never fully know. We only knew what we had experienced. That was the truth.

1835

"Ah, that feels great," I sighed as my husband rubbed the bottom of my foot firmly with his thumbs. I normally massaged him at the end of a hard day's work, but apparently he was in an extremely good mood today. As soon as we had sunk onto the couch after dinner, he had placed my feet on his lap and was demonstrating his amazing massage skills. It had been a while since I had felt so relaxed.

Especially with four children and a baby around us, moments of rest were very scarce. Right now the baby was sleeping and the rest were quietly playing upstairs. The fireplace was burning and created a cozy and warm feeling. That was a necessary thing for this cold house.

"I'll pay attention when you massage me, though." He leaned over and pressed a kiss to my forehead. I felt in love all over again. He was the best man I could wish for. Most of the time, that is. He had his moods, but everyone did, right?

I looked at his face. He was skinnier than most men I knew, but since he didn't do much physical labor, that made sense. Peter never had a big appetite either. Still, because of that, it was often thought that we were poor and had too little to eat. His eyes seemed just a bit too big for his face, but I had always liked that. They were almost the same shade of brown as his short hair. A beard had made his chin slightly darker since Johan was born.

On the floor above us, I suddenly heard quite a bit of rumbling and shouting. The girls were shouting at each other.

I frowned. "I think this means the end of our peace." I could have enjoyed this for hours, but duty called. "Let's put them to bed."

Peter hummed and gently removed my feet from his lap. Even before I could get up, he crawled across the couch to me and hovered diagonally above me. He pressed a kiss to my lips and whispered, "If they're in bed early, maybe we can practice for baby number six."

I giggled. "Petrus, Johan isn't even six weeks old yet."

"Hm, that's why I said practice."

Laughing, I pushed him off me and got up from the couch. He smiled back at me broadly, revealing his slightly yellowish teeth.

Hearing more screeching, I sighed and called out, "Aaltje, you shouldn't bully your sister like that." I ran up the stairs with my husband following me. Arriving in their bedroom, I saw what havoc had been wreaked. Their bedspread had been torn from their beds and all kinds of toys were scattered around the room. Aaltje's and Geertje's hair were tousled, as if it had been rooted through. I had heard a lot of rumbling, but nothing had indicated that this room was in such a bad state.

"What have you done?" I exclaimed, startled.

Geertje looked up at me with red eyes and tearful cheeks. "Aaltje hit me!" She pointed to her cheek, where indeed a red mark could be seen.

"But that's because Geertje scratched me!" Aaltje showed two deep red scratches running down her arm.

Indignation flooded my body, my face became warm. Sometimes I really wondered what was wrong with my girls. One minute they were angels and then they seemed to be taken over by the devil. I couldn't remember being like this with my sisters when I was young. Would other children in the village suffer from this too? Maybe it was because of our upbringing, I had to be even stricter with them. They couldn't keep hurting each other and others. Just like a few days ago, in the playground in the village. Then they had attacked a little boy with a stick. And before that, I had heard more often from parents that my girls were hurting their children.

"Mommy?" Dirk stood in the doorway. "I wanted to play with them, but they wouldn't let me." Bitterly he looked ahead of him.

I got up and walked toward him. My sons were always the victims of the girls' pranks. I couldn't stand it any longer. "I know, darling. Go to Peter and keep each other company. Mommy will be there in a minute to tuck you into bed."

He left the room, his footsteps dying away in the hallway. I turned back to my daughters and my husband. What was I going to do with my girls?

Petrus put an arm around my shoulders and pressed a firm kiss to my temple. Something about him had changed, but I couldn't put my finger on it. Every time he entered the room it was as if the air had become slightly more static, the world outside even darker. I shook off the feeling and forced a smile. I also had to keep myself big for the girls. They were too young to fully understand that their behavior was unacceptable.

"Just put the boys to bed, Esmeralda, and I'll take care of the girls." *You see,* I thought, *nothing to worry about.* His voice was quiet and calm. "Then I'll grab some wine from the cupboard and something to eat. I brought something home this afternoon as a surprise."

My heart made a jump. Whenever he brought something, it was usually another experience. It was often good food that we enjoyed. Or toys for the children, who then ran through the house for over an hour in joy. I couldn't wait to see what he had this time.

"Okay, see you in a bit."

The girls seemed to gravitate much more toward Petrus, and vice versa was true for the boys and me. They learned many things from their father, but when it came to the emotional bond, mine was stronger with the boys than with the girls. I hated to think of it that way, but it was true. I didn't dare talk about it with the other women in the village, afraid that what I was doing was completely wrong and that we would be gossiped about. So I didn't know if this was normal.

In the corridor I listened if there was any sound coming from our baby Johan's room. It was deadly quiet. It was great when he kept sleeping, even through the noise. Hopefully it would stay that way tonight. I walked on to the boys' bedroom, which was at the end of the landing on the right-hand side.

Affectionately, I looked at the picture before me.

Dirk was already in his pajamas and helping Peter do the same. What a good big brother he was. Both the boys looked up delightedly as I entered the bedroom.

"Mommy!"

"Hello boys, are we all ready for bed yet?"

They nodded proudly and both jumped into their own beds.

"Will you please tell a story?" Peter begged. Dirk nodded in agreement.

"Of course." I thought about a good story for a while and not much later I told them about a boy who lived in a dirty, old house. He had to help with a lot of chores that he actually wasn't very good at and because of that he was bullied by kids his age. His parents were often angry with him. He felt that he couldn't do anything, that nobody loved him. Eventually he found a very special talent that he was good at and he worked hard for it. He turned out to be one of the best furniture makers in the area and started a business, with people working for him. He made a lot of money, found a wonderful wife and built a beautiful house for his family, after which several children were born. They were very happy, but the man continued to work hard and he was often away from home. Still, he loved his family, even if he couldn't always show it.

"I think I already know who that story is about." Peter's head was only just poking out above the sheet.

"Oh, really?"

"Yes, about Dad!" His eyes twinkled at this discovery. Peter had never said much about his past, but this was all I knew about it. Besides, it was about the man he was now. You couldn't judge a man by his origins. I was a firm believer that people could change if they really tried. Especially with the right incentive.

I smiled and gave both my boys a kiss on their cheeks. "And now goodnight, darlings."

"Goodnight, Mom. Are we going to play outside together tomorrow?" Dirk asked.

"Of course, I would love that."

They nodded and closed their little eyes. I blew out the last oil lamps and their bedroom instantly became a lot darker.

"I love you," I whispered. I didn't know if they heard me, but I had to say it out loud.

I frowned when I heard Petrus walking up the stairs. Had he gone downstairs in the meantime? So why was he coming back up now? His footsteps went into the girls' room, after which I heard him mumble some things.

A nasty feeling settled in my lower abdomen. The feeling I had with him a moment ago was back.

On my guard I crept to the bedroom of Aaltje and Geertje on my toes. I thanked God that this house was solid and the wood did not creak under my feet as I crossed the landing. I stopped next to the doorway of their bedroom and pricked up my ears.

"You know this is your mother's fault, right?" I heard Petrus whisper.

Cautiously, I glanced around the corner. He was sitting on Aaltje's bed, stroking her hair. This gesture would have been endearing if such strange words had not come out of his mouth. Aaltje had her teddy bear pressed tightly against her and was looking at my husband with those big, innocent eyes of hers.

You see, they always listened better to Petrus. He had got them into their pajamas without any clear audible protest and they were lying quietly in bed.

Geertje, in the other bed, lay on her side and listened in amazement.

"Your mother hasn't been very kind, has she?" He affectionately ran a finger down her cheek.

Aaltje shook her head. "No, Mommy is mean."

"Yes, Mommy is mean. She loves Peter and Dirk much more than she loves you."

How dare he say that? We had talked so many times about how there was something wrong with Aaltje and Geertje and how I felt I couldn't connect with them. Was that why the girls always liked him more, because he manipulated them so much that they would hate me? No, I couldn't believe that. With open mouth I stared at the scene. Despite their problems, a mother's love knew no bounds. I loved them with all my heart. Why would Petrus say such a thing? What was he doing? He seemed out of sorts for a few days, but today he was his old self again. This really hit the spot.

"I will help you," he whispered.

His voice sounded so soft and so sweet that it gave me the shivers. Something was very wrong. Peter reached behind him and when his hand reappeared, something glinted in the moonlight. A knife.

I couldn't breathe, clutched at my chest. Was that what he had gone down for? What was he going to do with that knife? My whole body stiffened with fear.

"Daddy loves you girls. Are you going to help Daddy? This world is no place for special people like us. People don't understand us, we can have it much better." Peter raised the knife. "Don't be afraid, dear ones. And be quiet." He plunged the knife into her belly. A scream that was immediately smothered by his hand broke the silence of the night.

"No!" I shouted. My legs worked again and I stormed into the room. "Petrus, what are you doing?"

As soon as he caught sight of me, he removed his hand from Aaltje's lips and stood up. My little girl was breathing with shock, blood seeping from her mouth because of the internal injuries. Petrus looked straight at me. His eyes were insane. I hadn't seen him like that very often, but the times he had looked like that, he had been quite out of sorts. Then he was only after me, but he couldn't do this to the girls. And why were they lying there so quietly? My breathing quickened and my heart rate soared.

I pushed Peter aside and rushed to Aaltje. "Aaltje, darling." I pressed my hand to her stomach wound. "Mommy is here. Hang in there, sweetheart. We'll have the doctor come over. It was an accident."

Of course it wasn't an accident, but for her sake and maybe for my own, I wanted to keep up appearances. Her face grew whiter and whiter, her breathing shallower and shallower. Desperately I stared at her. There was nothing I could do except watch as my first child breathed her last breath in my arms. I didn't have a chance to shed a tear before my shoulders were yanked and I fell backwards, onto my back. I quickly scrambled to my feet and looked up at my husband.

"What have you done?" I shouted. A flame was brewing inside me, a primal force, more powerful than I had ever felt it.

"I relieved them from their suffering. From your clutches!"

"What do you mean?" He was crazy. What was he doing?

"You love Dirk and Peter more than your daughters. They are going under, going crazy in their heads because of the lack of love I can't give them either. They don't belong in this world, would never be happy there. This is better for them." He towered at least a head above me and looked up and down menacingly. My eyes shot to the blood-covered knife he held in his hands and I took a step back.

"You're crazy!" I exclaimed. "How is this the solution? Yes, they are suffering from hysteria, but there is nothing they can do about it. Just like you!" It had been clear to me for some time that their behavior was much like what their father sometimes displayed.

"How dare you say I am sick in the head, woman? You were having sex with another man behind my back!"

"What man? Petrus, what are you talking about?" I wanted to rant, cry and roar, but instead I looked at my Aaltje. Her eyes stared lifelessly at the ceiling. She was nothing more than a rag doll. Geertje. My dear Geertje had seen all this. But when I looked at her, I did not see what I expected. She was not crying, not screaming. She was still lying there looking, a smile played around her mouth.

"And they obviously got that disease from you!" I spat at his feet. "You're crazy!" I repeated.

With the handle of the knife he gave me such a hard blow against the side of my head that everything went black for a moment. I lost my balance and sank to my knees.

"Geertje, my girl," he said endearingly. "Do you want to be with your sister?"

"Yes, Daddy."

What was wrong with them? That was all I could think as I lay helpless on the floor. These girls were defenseless.

"No, Petrus! Please, we can fix this. We can get you some help. And for them...her." My voice sounded hoarse, no more than a whisper, but he had heard me.

"Quiet! You will suffer the consequences of your actions." With large strides he walked towards Geertje. Without another word and with a cloudy look in his eyes he put the knife to her throat. And he cut. A gurgling sound, like a stifled moan, sounded from her throat. Her body cramped and her hands balled into fists.

At that moment, it felt like my heart was being ripped from my chest. My breath was taken away from me. An icy cry left my throat, screeched across the mountains.

He stomped across the room and stopped next to Aaltje's bed. "This is your fault, Esmeralda!" As if in a burst of rage, he lashed out with his fist and slammed into the first thing he could find: Aaltje's face. A loud crack was the result and her jaw had landed at an odd angle.

Paralyzed, I looked at my children. My little girls. I gave birth to them. Raised them with so much love. Taken away from me by the man I had first loved so much.

"Mama?"

I turned abruptly to the doorway and was immediately on my feet. "Dirk, get Peter and hide. Now!" I shouted. "Get your little brother and get out of this house."

It was obvious he didn't understand why I said that. He wanted to know what was going on. But the look in my eyes compelled him to. He turned and ran out of sight.

"I didn't think so!" Petrus shouted. "Dirk, stand down immediately!"

Fortunately, he wasn't listening to his father.

Before Petrus had a chance to walk onto the landing, I blocked his way. My heart made a jump when I looked into his eyes. Hard, cold, emotionless. He really had lost his way completely.

"No, I won't let you do this. You can't."

He tilted his head. "You see, even now you don't protect your daughters, but you do protect your sons. Just like my mother didn't care about me or my brothers, but she did care about my sisters."

"You do this because you supposedly didn't get enough love from your mother? You know she loved you dearly," I tried to soothe him.

"Out of the way!" Roughly he pushed me away from him.

I stumbled after him as he caught up with Dirk, still seeing black spots appear before my eyes from time to time. I quickened my pace and when I reached out my hand, I could almost touch Petrus. Before that happened, however, he rammed the knife into Dirk's back with one swipe. Dirk stopped in mid-stride; as if stiffened, he stood in the hallway. When Petrus pulled out the knife, he collapsed.

"Peter, no!" My cry had to be heard for miles around. My heart was torn to pieces. Every time my husband took the lives of my children, another piece of my heart broke.

This time I did manage to grab him by the arm. I squeezed as hard as I could, drilling my hands into his skin. Blood flowed along my nails and I slapped his wrist, trying to get that knife out of his hands in any way I could. My husband, however, was much bigger and stronger than I was, so it didn't take him long to free himself from my grip and slam me against the wall with ferocious force. The back of my head slammed against the wall. Red spots appeared in my field of vision. Through them I saw him walking toward the boys' bedrooms.

I clung to Petrus' arm once more. "Petrus, no."

"I don't care how many times you say that, shrew. You are responsible for this. For you, I have something special in store," he hissed at me.

Startled, I let go of his arm. I could not stop him. I

was too weak, too small, too broken. Yet I ran after him. I hit him several times on his back, my feet against his legs. It didn't bother him.

Just before we entered the room, he hit me so hard in the face that I fell to the floor. Again. It was too much, the blows I had received against my head. I couldn't manage to get up. All I could do was stay down. Waiting. Hearing how the knife cut through bone and skin. How little Peter screamed, how it was stifled. Until then it was completely silent.

With a bloodied knife, Petrus walked out of their room, heading for the next room.

"No, not Johan! He's just a baby, he's not aware of any wrongdoing!" I called after him.

He ignored me, did not respond to my plea. From the room came the sound that resembled the beginning of a cry, but it stopped abruptly. My last child had been taken from me. The last time I was with Johan, he made laughing sounds, but his crying at his father was the last I heard of him.

Petrus stormed out of the room, my way, grabbed my arm roughly and dragged me down the stairs, to the basement door. Meanwhile, I begged him not to go through with this. Why I did that, I didn't know. After all this, I had nothing left to live for. My life had been destroyed. Drastically changed in less than ten minutes.

He opened the basement door, pushed me in front of him, and then pulled the door shut behind him. He forced me down the stairs. I descended further and further into the darkness. I couldn't see a hand in front of me. Foot by foot I shuffled forward. I felt the paralyzing feeling of fear spreading through my body. It made my legs go numb and I began to sweat profusely.

His hand on my back urged me to continue walking. The push caused me to fall forward and I almost tripped over an object that was in my way. Petrus roughly grabbed the top of my dress and forced me to stand up, pulling me against him. His hand rubbed up my back, to my neck, where his fingers touched my skin. The compelling feeling of his fingers crept up to my throat. With the knife, he scratched a shallow slit in my skin, gently and cautiously. The silent warning could not be clear enough.

I swallowed. Suppressed the urge to sprint away and run, far away from him, because I knew that I would meet my end immediately. Sadness flooded me as I thought back to what had happened up there. I had been powerless, no matter how hard I tried.

Petrus lit a candle that was always in the basement, through which I could see the dust swirling down around us. With a compelling motion, he led me through the dusty basement. In no million years had I thought he would be capable of something so gruesome that even the dead turned over in their graves.

At the very back of the basement he came to a stop. Petrus placed the candle on a coffin and moved the cabinet.

My body felt like it was frozen. I touched my skin. It was cold. I couldn't feel my lips moving as I tried to form words, so I said nothing.

I took a small step backwards, with difficulty. Only then did I notice how uncontrollably I was shaking.

"Stay back!" he growled.

Without thinking, I did as he said. As I always did. And it was precisely in this state that I better listen to him.

With heavy panting and a whole lot of moaning, he moved the cabinet inch by inch. When the cabinet was out of the way, he picked up the candle.

The light showed me a square piece of wall that looked different from the others. He looked up at me, a big grin marring his face. Normally I loved that smile, but now he was scaring me in a way I didn't know before.

He punched the brick, which crumbled. He grabbed my arm and pushed me out in front of him into a dark room. A hallway. I had no idea we had a hallway like this under our house.

I didn't want to realize it, but deep down I knew I was facing my death. I knew that from the moment he had drilled the knife into Aaltje. My Aaltje, Geertje, Peter, Dirk and Johan. If only I could be with you. If only I could have protected you against the wrath of your father.

We walked through the dark corridor, which opened into another, square room.

"What are you up to, Petrus?" I dared to ask.

"Shut up, woman."

I pressed my lips together.

Petrus pulled me toward him and pushed me into a corner of the room. His face was close to mine as he spoke. "You will never be found. People will think that you killed your family. That you are the culprit. Which is true, of course, but sometimes people need an extra push to believe that." Saliva splashed my face as he spoke. "You demoness."

Finally I let my tears flow. There was nowhere to gain honor from this situation. "Petrus, we've been together so long..."

"That doesn't matter."

And before I could say another word, before I could get him to change his mind while sobbing, I felt a hellish stab in my chest. The knife pierced my lung, I felt it. At first, I couldn't believe it, I thought I could resist it, my approaching death. Just keep breathing. Just keep living. Stay alive to let the world know what Petrus had done, who the real culprit was here. I had to. But soon the darkness set in. It swallowed me up. Every time I blinked, Peter's face became blurrier. Until the darkness embraced me completely.

Acknowledgements

What started as a few nightmares and my own fears, has grown into an actual book! There are so many people who have helped and supported me throughout the entire process.

Firstly, I want to thank my publisher: Hamley Books. Sandra and Cathy, thank you so much for your trust in this story and the opportunity.

Secondly, AM Ink, thank you for giving *In the Dark* a chance in the US! It's a wild dream come true as a small Dutch author.

Lotte van den Noort, my Hamley Books colleague, thank you for being my beta reader. And I'm sorry for the sleepless night afterwards. You are a real friend and you have helped me so much.

Valentijn Ringelberg, also my Hamley Books colleague, thank you for reading the first draft and for the messages that always made me laugh my ass off.

Juliëtte Heugen, I want to thank you for your friendship and the messages that gave me new insights. Keep writing the books you're writing, I love them!

Of course I want to thank all my beta readers: Lotte van den Noort, Ruby Coene-Pothoven, Sanne

Hillemans, Anastasia Sidiropoulou, Maartje Mijnen, Cindy Pel and Suzanne Kol. Thank you so much for your input and critique. I may have cried a little bit, but the story has gotten so much better!

Maud Vosselman, my high school Dutch teacher, thank you for reading the manuscript that came before *In the Dark* and for your enthusiasm of the Dutch language.

I want to thank my families and friends. You don't always get what I love so much about reading and writing, but you are always by my side, supporting me.

And you, reader of *In the Dark*, are helping me make a dream come true. Because without you, this story cannot come alive! So, thank you!

About the Author

Tamara Arts (2000) has been writing her whole life. Currently she is studying to become a Dutch teacher, in the hopes of making her students enthusiastic about the Dutch language. In her free time, she enjoys going to the gym, read and meet up with friends.

For more about Tamara Arts, visit:

www.tamaraarts.nl

www.ingramcontent.com/pod-product-compliance
Lightning Source LLC
Chambersburg PA
CBHW030246030726
47493CB00023B/872